Meet Pe

Her special c...
is launc...

Penny has been writing exclusively for
Mills & Boon® for twenty years, from her
home in Cheshire where she lives with her
husband, three dogs, and two cats. Brought up in
Preston, Lancashire, Penny's family moved to
Cheshire when she was seventeen. She started her
working life as a secretary in a bank, but had always
told and written stories for herself and her family.

After reading an article in a magazine about
how Mills & Boon were looking for new writers, she
submitted a story just out of curiosity. With very few
amendments, that first submission was published,
and one hundred novels later, what started as a
hobby is now a way of life.

'All my books are special at the time of writing,'
says Penny, 'which means I don't have favourites.
I have left it up to the editors at Mills & Boon to tell
me which have been most popular,
and which should go into the
Collector's Edition, because what
matters is what my readers like.'

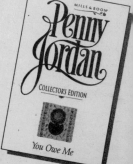

*Look out for this exciting
'Collector's Edition' over
the coming months*

'Teddy?' he called out

She stood under a steady stream, unmoving, her head tilted back as she let the water run over her. It was almost as if she had been expecting him. Wanting him as much as he wanted her.

Mack took in the vision of Teddy standing in the shower, naked and wet before him, more beautiful than he ever remembered, and he knew there was no turning back. He saw the slight smile on her lips—seductive, anxious, knowing. She reached out, snatched the edge of his shirt between her fingers and drew him slowly towards her. Silently she undid each button and tugged the ends free from his jeans.

Her eyes never left his. Even when she pushed back his shirt, dropping it to the floor, and trailed her wet fingers down his torso, her silvery gaze held his. When she reached for the snap on his jeans, Mack's breath caught in his throat.

'Are you coming in?' she murmured. 'Or do I have to come out and get you?'

To Brenda Chin
editor *and* friend.

And to Andrea Wyman,
a constant and reliable source of euphemisms.

For **Morgan Hayes,** the idea of setting a story in the
Colorado Rockies was too good to pass up. After all, what
woman hasn't dreamed of being snowbound in a mountain
cabin with a sexy stranger? And how many of us haven't,
at least once in our lives, thought about running away
from it all? Just to disappear for a few weeks... What
Morgan hadn't counted on was the explosive chemistry
that developed between her characters. 'But then again—'
she laughs 'it *is* a Temptation®!'

SEDUCED BY A STRANGER

BY

MORGAN HAYES

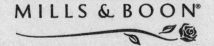

MILLS & BOON®

*MILLS & BOON and MILLS & BOON with the Rose Device
are registered trademarks of the publisher.
TEMPTATION is a registered trademark of
Harlequin Enterprises Limited, used under licence.*

*First published in Great Britain 1998
by Harlequin Mills & Boon Limited,
Eton House, 18-24 Paradise Road, Richmond, Surrey TW9 1SR*

© Illona Haus 1997

ISBN 0 263 81128 X

21-9806

*Printed and bound in Great Britain
by Caledonian International Book Manufacturing Ltd, Glasgow*

1

SO WHAT WAS A NICE woman like Teddy Logan doing in a place like this? Mack Carlino wondered again. From where he sat at a scarred table by the door of Sly's Tavern, his hands wrapped around a mug of coffee, Mack had a clear view of the bar.

The place was nothing beyond typical. A dozen patrons warmed the stools, bellying up to their accustomed Tuesday-night beers. Their laughter rose over some country-and-western song on the jukebox as they bantered about the weather, the faltering economy and the hockey highlights that flickered on the small TV mounted in the corner.

Nothing unusual.

Past the smoke-shrouded dimness, Mack looked to the expanse of mahogany and mirrors of the bar. A thin strand of age-old tinsel wrapped around the brass railing was the last vestige of Christmas, and a plastic Happy New Year's sign hung lopsided by one thread from the lighted canopy.

You couldn't find a more typical small-town watering hole than Sly's Tavern, Mack thought. Except for one thing—the woman who served up drinks on the other side of the bar. The woman Mack had been searching for.

Teddy Logan.

Through a blue veil of cigarette smoke, her easy smile glowed—a soft, sensuous smile that started at the corners of those lush lips and reached up into her bright eyes. A smile both honest and inviting, yet at the same time concealing a thousand secrets—secrets that belonged to a world far removed from this one-tavern mountain town of Birdseye, Colorado.

From the second he'd walked through the door and kicked the snow off his boots an hour ago, Mack had been watching her. He liked to think that he couldn't take his eyes off her because he'd been paid to, that after finally finding her, he was not about to lose sight of Teddy Logan again. But there was more to it than that. The ache in his groin proved it.

Mack shifted in his seat, wishing he could look away. But he couldn't.

He caught the gentle lilt of her laughter, and watched her shake her head at one of the patrons before sliding him another beer with all the skill of a seasoned bartender. Mack hadn't been surprised at the number of men who had come on to her in the short time he'd been here. Even if he *hadn't* been looking for Teddy Logan, Mack knew that his gaze, like many others tonight, would have been riveted on the stunning blonde behind the bar.

Funny thing was, he didn't like blondes, as a rule. Growing up in the back streets of New York City's Little Italy, he'd always found himself drawn to the darker, more exotic look.

Maybe it was the lighting, the way her hair shone like pale liquid gold under the dim overhead lights and her perfect skin radiated a softness that made Mack wonder how it might feel under his fingertips. Or maybe it was the way she moved—her gestures so fluid, the alluring curves of her slender frame seductively revealed by the formfitting top she wore with snug jeans. He imagined running his hand along those curves.

Twice Mack had seen her step out from behind the bar: once to speak with the waitress, and again to slip into the kitchen. Both times his gaze had studied...no, caressed each delicious line of her enticing figure. And he imagined that figure in something more along the lines of what Teddy Logan would normally wear, something expensive, something slinky yet classy. A short black cocktail dress would be stunning, Mack thought, with nothing but sheer stockings on those long legs. Or maybe even something a bit more tempting, more silky, with a touch of lace and less—

A blast of frigid air swept through the door as two patrons bustled in from the storm. And with the rush of cold air came Mack's sense of reason. He had to keep his mind on his job, he scolded himself. This was *not* the time to indulge in torrid fantasies—especially those involving the fiancée of his client.

He watched the two men cross to the bar where Teddy had their beers already waiting. She knew them. In fact, she seemed to know most of the customers, and yet she'd been in Birdseye for less than two weeks by Mack's estimation.

It had taken him a week to track her down—through three different states and twice as many cities, only to find her here, back in Colorado, less than four hours from her home. And in the time he'd been searching for her, Teddy Logan had not only gotten herself this job, but she even knew what the locals drank.

Mack reached into the pocket of his leather jacket draped over the chair and pulled out the three-by-five glossy he'd been carrying for the past week—a photo of Teddy. It had been taken last fall, her fiancé had told him when he'd handed Mack the picture, back in Denver. And from that first glance at the photo, Mack had been struck by Teddy Logan's natural beauty—a low afternoon sun warmed her fair complexion, and a breeze tugged at long wisps of golden hair and at the white shirt she wore tucked into a pair of suede riding chaps. In one hand she held a helmet and a crop, while in the other she gripped the bridle of a tall, chestnut horse.

But it was Teddy's eyes that had haunted Mack—eyes the color of the sea, a cold and piercing slate blue. Yet there was a warmth to them, a radiance that had made him wonder about the woman behind that vibrant smile. And, yes, he'd wondered about her a lot during the last few days.

"Hey, Teddy!" one of the men at the bar called out.

Mack glanced up from the picture.

"Teddy, I gotta tell ya, honey, and this ain't just the beer talkin', okay?" the man went on. "But I gotta say, I always fancied me marrying a bartender, ya know?"

"Is that right, Joe?"

Mack watched her set two beers on the waitress's tray before turning to her most recent suitor. She planted her hands on her slim hips and faced him with one of her brilliant smiles.

"Yup, it's the God-honest truth," Joe answered her. "Ask Dwayne here. Haven't I always said that?"

His friend only shook his head with an embarrassed grin.

"I always said that one day...one day I'd find me a good-looking bartender, and then I'd marry her. So waddaya say, Teddy? Huh?"

"Well, Joe." She put away several empties, and ran a rag over the length of the bar. "If marrying a bartender is your goal in life, then far be it from me to stop you." Amusement never left her lips. "In fact, since my shift is over, I'll tell you what I'll do for you, Joe. Sly should be here any second. I can talk to him. See what he says. But I'll be straight with you...I really don't think you're his type."

"Ah, Teddy, yer breakin' my heart, you know that?"

"I think you'll get over it, Joe. No doubt by the time you see the bottom of that beer."

Mack swilled the last of his coffee and saw the playful

wink she gave the man as she finished wiping down the bar. She was smooth. Mack had to give her that. And he certainly didn't blame the guy for trying. If *he'd* been the one with a few beers in his belly instead of this coffee, he might have been inclined to make a proposal himself to a woman like Teddy Logan. Still, Mack couldn't suppress an unexpected twinge of jealousy, as if he somehow had a prior claim on Teddy. After all, hadn't she been his singular focus for the better part of this past week?

"You want a refill on that, hon?"

Abruptly Mack closed his hand over Teddy's photo and returned it to his jacket pocket, praying that the wide-eyed waitress standing next to his table hadn't seen it. He gazed up at her, noticing her cluttered tray propped against one small hip as she looked at him expectantly.

"It's a cold one out there," she reminded him. "Did you want another coffee?"

"No." He pushed the empty cup across the table along with his dinner plate, and took out his wallet. "No, thanks. I'm fine. What do I owe you?"

"Six-eighty."

Mack handed her a ten. "Keep the change."

"Thanks." She slipped the bill into her apron and gathered his dishes. "You're not from around here, are you?" she asked.

"No."

"Didn't think so." The waitress chattered on, but Mack only half listened. As she loaded her tray, his gaze was drawn, almost involuntarily, to Teddy once again. She was speaking with an older man now behind the bar. The man's ruddy face was circled by a full head of shocking-white hair and a thick beard to match. When he wore that red flannel shirt, Mack guessed the man took his share of Santa-related gibes, especially this time of the year.

"So what brings you to Birdseye?" the waitress asked.

"Nothing. Just passing through." He pocketed his wallet and reached for his jacket. It appeared as though Teddy was making moves to leave.

"I thought maybe you were a skier. We get a lot of them up here," the waitress said. "Renting the cabins up the mountain. You planning on staying in Birdseye long?"

"No. Like I said, I'm passing through."

"Well, you'd better think twice about 'passing through' in this storm, hon. The boys say it's turning right miserable out there. Probably even worse farther up the mountain. You'll wanna be careful driving."

"Thanks. I will."

"Come on, Maryanne. We got drinks stacking up here," the Santa-look-alike shouted to her.

The waitress gave him a quick wave and gathered her tray. "That's my cue." She rolled her eyes. "Take care, ya hear?"

Mack waited until she left his table before he stood. Shrugging his jacket onto his shoulders, he glanced once more to the bar. But this time Teddy caught his stare. Her gaze locked with his, and he could almost feel those blue-gray eyes sweep over him, cooling his heated thoughts.

And then she smiled. A quiet smile, barely perceptible on her lips, but he saw it touch the corners of her eyes. Mack groaned inwardly. Under any other circumstances, he would have gone straight to the bar and taken her up on that enchanting invitation. He would have introduced himself, bought her a drink, maybe even asked her to share a dance with him on the small floor in front of the jukebox. He'd hold her close, feel those enticing curves he'd admired for the past hour press against his body, and then—

No! He couldn't think like this. He couldn't afford mistakes. He was here on an assignment. He'd been hired to find Teddy Logan, and he'd done just that. He should go to the pay phone at the back and call Denver right now. In fact, he should have called an hour ago when he'd first laid eyes on her.

He didn't know why he felt compelled to hold off. But he knew that he had questions—questions that only Teddy Logan could answer. And this was hardly the place.

TEDDY WATCHED the stranger flip up the collar of his leather bomber jacket and turn, rather abruptly, she thought. For a moment she'd caught his penetrating gaze—eyes as dark as his sleek, jet-black hair—and she'd half expected him to approach the bar and introduce himself. Instead he'd headed for the door, and in seconds was lost in a flurry of snow.

An hour ago, when the stranger had first walked in, he'd immediately caught Teddy's attention, but she had limited her curiosity to only occasional glances while she tended bar. Still, she'd seen enough to recognize that he wasn't from Birdseye, nor was he one of the tourists who braved the unpredictable mountain conditions for the well-guarded secret of prime ski slopes.

He'd been too groomed, with his expensive haircut and fine leather jacket. In spite of his five o'clock shadow, the rumpled shirt and the creased but snug jeans, Teddy figured him as the kind of man who took pride in his appearance, and who would not normally have come into a bar looking as scruffy as he'd been tonight. He'd had "big city" written all over him, and in between serving beers, Teddy had spent part of her evening wondering what had brought this stranger through Birdseye in the first place.

It was a game she'd played many times while behind the bar—here now and once years ago—imagining the lives of the patrons who came and went. It had started back in college, when she'd taken to bartending as something of a diversion rather than a job. She hadn't needed the money then; no, her father had seen to it that all of her expenses were met, including the BMW, the Manhattan apartment and unlimited return flights to Denver so she could come home for visits. Not that she'd often bothered.

Back then, she'd taken to bartending more as a means of maintaining her sanity, to get out, to meet people, to escape her studies. To be normal. But now, here in Birdseye, tending bar was a job. Teddy needed the money. And fortunately Sly didn't mind paying her in cash.

She'd been straight with Sly from the start—told him she needed the job and had the experience, but admitted that she wasn't certain how long she could stay. She'd been passing through, or so she'd thought, on her way to God-knows-where, when the storm had hit. Seeing the welcome lights of Birdseye, she'd decided it was best not to tempt fate. She'd parked the Jeep outside the main-street tavern and gone in.

Sly seemed to recognize she was in trouble, and hadn't demanded an explanation or references. And before the evening was out, the snowy-haired proprietor had offered her a job and his rental cabin up the mountain. Teddy was grateful for his trust.

"Teddy?"

She wasn't sure how long she'd been standing there, with an empty beer bottle in each hand, staring after the stranger, but it must have been awhile because Sly's voice held a tone of concern.

"Teddy? Are you all right?"

"Yes. Yes, Sly." She dragged her gaze from the door where only moments ago the handsome stranger had stood. "I'm fine."

"I asked if you were going to the cabin or if you'd prefer to stay in town tonight. The storm's picking up. You're welcome at my place if you like."

"No, I'll be all right, Sly, thanks. I'll get through. Besides, I've got to feed Bogie." She thought of the hungry malamute that would be greeting her the second she stepped through the cabin door.

"Well, drive careful then."

"I will, Sly." She smiled at his concern, and stashed the last empty under the bar. Less than two weeks and it already felt as if Sly and this bar had been a part of her life forever. In fact, Birdseye was starting to feel more like home than Denver ever had.

"Good night, Sly. I'll see you tomorrow," she said, starting to the kitchen door.

But when Sly said good-night, he did not do so alone. The dozen or so regulars hunkered around the bar also shouted farewells to Teddy as if she'd worked here all her life, as though she was the only person who had ever slid them a beer down this bar. She smiled, shouldered her purse and gave them a wave.

At the back door, Teddy changed into her snow boots and bundled into her fleece-lined Gore-Tex coat. She was prepared for the worst, but when she stepped out of the shelter of the passageway behind Sly's place, the full extent of the storm wasn't immediately evident. And it certainly wasn't enough to keep Maryanne from sneaking a quick cigarette.

"So you're heading out in this crap?" Maryanne asked, taking a long drag before pulling her bare hands deeper into the sleeves of her oversize parka.

Teddy nodded, and glanced across the snow-blown parking lot to her half-buried Jeep. "You can bet tonight's tips I am," she said with a smile. "There's a long hot bath waiting for me up that mountain, with my name in bubbles."

Teddy caught the glint of envy in the other woman's eyes. "Well, at least *one* of us can get out of here at a decent hour."

Maryanne savored her last drag and flicked the butt into the snow. "Me, I'm here to the bitter end."

"Oh, come on, Maryanne, you're just sore because your mystery man didn't ask for your number before he left."

"*My* number? Hon, if you're referring to the dark-haired Adonis at the far table tonight, I don't think it was *my* number he was after. In case you hadn't noticed, Mr. Italian-Stallion was checking *you* out the entire time."

"Me? I hardly think so." Teddy laughed as she dug into her coat pocket for her car keys.

"Oh, don't give me that Ms. Innocent routine," Maryanne teased. "I saw you watching him."

Teddy couldn't escape Maryanne's infectious smile, nor could she deny the truth. She *had* noticed the stranger, and his incredible physique, from his broad shoulders to his narrow waist. "All right, fine. I admit it, I did sort of look at the guy."

"Too bad he's just passing through, huh?"

"You asked?" Teddy heard surprise in her own voice.

"What? You honestly think I'd let him leave *without* asking?"

Teddy shook her head, smiling. "And here I thought you were a happily married woman."

"Oh, sure I am. But a girl can still look, can't she? Besides, I was checking him out for you, Teddy. You think I didn't notice that you're not wearing that engagement ring anymore?"

Teddy clenched her car keys in her gloved hand, and felt the unfamiliar nakedness of her ring finger. She'd taken Alan's ring off last week, figuring that no one had noticed it yet, and that she would raise fewer eyebrows at the bar without the ostentatious diamond on her hand.

"Well, I'm sorry to disappoint you, Maryanne, but I'm not in the market."

"Fine then," Maryanne said finally, reaching for the door handle. "If you say so."

Teddy was certain she'd heard disappointment in the other woman's voice, and again regretted the secrecy she'd had to maintain since her arrival in Birdseye. She hated lying to Maryanne and the others. But living a lie was the only way Teddy could stay in Birdseye, the only way she could protect her anonymity, and the only way to maintain her distance from Alan.

"Good luck getting to the cabin," Maryanne shouted over her shoulder as she swung open the back door.

"Good night, Maryanne." Teddy gazed from the keys in her hand to the Jeep at the other side of the lot. In the glow of the lamp overhead, she watched the wind whip thick snowflakes into a glittering whirlwind.

Yes, it bothered Teddy to lie, to hide the truth from the people she'd begun to care about. But it was too soon. She wasn't ready to go back to Denver. She wasn't ready to go back to Alan. Not yet. And maybe never.

FROM BEHIND the wheel of his Mustang, Mack looked out across the parking lot of Sly's Tavern. He'd had the engine running until the waitress had come out for her smoke. Now, through a dusting of snow on the windshield, he could just make out Teddy's solitary figure against a swirl of white.

The waitress had gone back inside, and for a long moment Teddy just stood there, staring out into the night. Mack wondered what she saw there, if anything.

Finally she crossed the lot to the black Wrangler, and unlocked the door. Mack leaned forward in his seat to watch her, one gloved hand toying with the key chain that hung from the Mustang's ignition. As soon as she started the Jeep, he'd turn over his own engine. Not before. He couldn't alert her to his presence.

He watched her hop into the driver's seat, and in seconds he heard the roar of the Jeep. A plume of blue smoke hung momentarily in the freezing air behind it.

Mack started the Mustang. He flicked the windshield wipers once, and watched her brush off her vehicle, but the snow seemed to fall and settle almost as quickly as she could sweep it.

It wasn't until he shoved the car into gear and pulled out of the parking lot at a safe enough distance behind her that Mack realized the insanity of what he was doing. Driving up the near-empty main street of Birdseye, heading north out of town, he now had a truer picture of the storm. He'd be lucky to make it up the mountain in the Mustang under these conditions.

He should have just checked into the hotel at the other end of town and not worried about making contact until tomorrow, when the weather cleared. But Mack couldn't risk waiting that long. He'd spent a week finding Teddy Logan, and he couldn't risk losing her now. Besides, he had too many questions.

Sure, he'd been hired to find her, report her location to her fiancé—that was all. But there were pieces to this puzzle that were missing, and he needed answers that only Teddy could give him. From the start, Mack had had a bad feeling about this job and about his client Alan Somerton. Twelve years as a cop had trained Mack to listen to his inner voice, and right now that voice was telling him to get Teddy's side of the story before doing anything else. Then again, considering the titillating daydreams he'd succumbed to at the bar, Mack could only wonder which voice he was listening to right now.

The Jeep's taillights were wavering points of red through

the driving snow, threatening to vanish altogether. Still, Mack lagged behind as far as he dared. There was no doubt that she would see his headlights in her rearview mirror, and he needed to avoid suspicion as long as possible. She'd likely become wary as soon as they hit the remote side roads farther up the mountain.

Just this afternoon, Mack had inquired at the gas station about the various rental cabins in the area, figuring that Teddy had likely taken one for herself. He'd found out about the cabin owned by Sly Valeriano, the owner of the bar, and he'd even managed to get general directions. Still, in this storm, Mack couldn't risk losing sight of Teddy's Jeep. It wouldn't take much to become hopelessly lost.

He reached for the radio, and cranked the volume. Over the roar of the Mustang's dash fans and the scudding of wipers across the icy windshield, The Zombies wailed out "Time of the Season." They were far enough out of Birdseye now that Mack knew Teddy had to be questioning the headlights in her rearview mirror. What if she suspected her fiancé was trying to find her? Teddy Logan had already proven she didn't want to be found. She'd managed to stump Mack for a week, leaving him with dead ends and only the most limited of leads as to her whereabouts. She'd taken sanctuary in this town, fitting in like a chameleon, and she was hardly about to blow that well-devised cover. If Teddy was as smart as Mack gave her credit for, surely she'd notice a vehicle tailing her along a deserted mountain road in the dead of night.

No sooner had these thoughts flashed through Mack's mind when suddenly the Jeep was gone. In the glare of the Mustang's headlights, gusts of snow swept the drifted road ahead of him. Beyond that, there was only blackness.

He sat up straighter and dared to give the car more gas.

He couldn't have lost her. It was impossible! She couldn't be there one second and gone the next.

And then, with a sigh of relief, Mack saw the shimmering red glow once again. But the Jeep was picking up speed. The taillights were pulling away at a steady rate, and unless he pushed the low-riding Mustang to its limit, Mack really *was* going to lose her.

2

THE STRANGER from the bar had been on Teddy's mind from the moment she'd left. And Maryanne's words had repeated themselves in her head, lending an involuntary curve to Teddy's lips as she drove out of Birdseye. She'd spent the next fifteen minutes remembering the man's dark gaze across the bar, the way her heart had raced when those mysterious eyes locked with hers.

And when she had turned the Jeep off the main road and headed north, Teddy had been wondering about the man in the rumpled shirt and faded jeans. She'd gripped the steering wheel firmly in both hands as the vehicle bounced through mounting snowdrifts, but her mind was toying with images of the tall stranger. She wished she'd had the nerve to go up to him at the end of her shift, introduce herself and say whatever it was that women said to pick up men in bars. It was completely out of character for her, something she'd never have dreamed of doing back in Denver, with Alan still in her life. But now, miles away from all of that, Teddy could almost imagine the flirtatious conversation they might have shared. And she could easily imagine those dark eyes gazing into hers.

Teddy squinted against a sudden glare, her daydream shattered. The headlights were there again, in her rearview mirror. She'd noticed them shortly after leaving the back lot of Sly's, and had tried to quell her suspicions. But after turning off Birdseye's main street and seeing the headlights still behind her, those suspicions no longer seemed unfounded.

For a while, she'd thought she'd lost the vehicle. But it was still there, hanging back just far enough for her to believe that the driver was trying to be inconspicuous. "Inconspicuous," however, was hardly possible here in the Colorado Rockies, where the narrow roads twisted and turned their way up the mountain.

No. One thing was for damned sure. She was being tailed.

And Teddy had a pretty good idea who was behind the wheel of that vehicle. Or, at least, who had hired him.

Alan.

It didn't matter that she'd called Alan three weeks ago to tell him she was all right. She'd barely said hello into the frozen mouthpiece of the pay phone outside the gas station in Richfield, when Alan had demanded to know where she was and when she'd be home. And Teddy had known he was biting his tongue throughout their brief conversation, ready to blow up at her. That was why she'd hung up. And the reason she hadn't contacted him again.

When she telephoned her friend Holly in Fort Collins a week later, Teddy wasn't surprised to hear that Alan had been calling everyone she knew, claiming he was frantic to find her. It was then that Teddy stopped using her credit cards.

She wasn't ready to return to Denver yet. *Or* to talk to Alan.

The last time she'd seen him, she'd been in his office, a month ago, at her father's company, Logan Publishing. She'd wrapped up early with an editorial meeting and had gone to find Alan, but when he wasn't in his office, she'd decided to wait. Sitting at his desk for less than a minute, Teddy knew she'd seen things on his computer screen that Alan undoubtedly hadn't wanted her to see. Things that she didn't entirely comprehend even now, but might have figured out if she hadn't been interrupted by Alan's arrival.

The second he came through the door, Alan had made a beeline toward her. He'd leaned across the desk, placing a kiss on her lips as though he was delighted to see her, but Teddy had heard him finger the keyboard. And when Alan pulled away from her at last, the computer screen was blank, the columns of figures gone.

She'd asked him about what she'd seen, why he'd been accessing the Logan accounts, and in retrospect, Teddy wished she'd pressed him further on the issue. But Alan's defensiveness had startled her. Whatever it was Alan was up to, Teddy probably could have accepted, but his reaction—the tone of accusation that had sharpened his voice when he suggested she'd been snooping into his private files—for Teddy, that had been the last straw in their already shaky engagement.

She could still picture the way the muscle along his jaw had clenched, how his hands had balled into white-knuckled fists at his side. And she could still remember his response when she'd told him she was leaving.

"What? You're going to up and leave? Just like that?" he'd asked. His jaw tightened again, and Teddy had been surprised at how his usually handsome features contorted into something she hardly recognized. "Teddy, we've got the Sandler project to wrap up, and you've got meetings with writers and agents clear through to the end of next month. You can't just—"

"Watch me, Alan." She'd started for the door, but in a flash his hand had snaked over and caught her arm. He'd twisted her around to face him, and Teddy was shocked by the unfamiliar fury she saw there.

"Teddy, think of the company. You can't leave like this."

"Alan, let go of me." His hand had become a vise, biting into the soft flesh of her arm. But he didn't release her.

"Teddy, whatever you saw...whatever you *think* you saw—"

"Does it matter?"

He was speechless.

"Does it honestly matter what I saw in here, Alan?"

"You can't leave, Teddy. Not now. There's too much at stake. The company—"

"I don't owe this company anything!" Her own pent-up anger had surprised her. "I gave up my law degree for this company. I dropped everything at Yale and came back here when my father had his heart attack. I put everything on hold for him, and three years later, I'm still here." Years of bitterness broke through. Years of watching her mother succumb to the cancer that finally took her life when Teddy was only thirteen, years of watching her father bury himself in his work...

Logan Publishing. It was always Logan Publishing—the company Teddy had come to both love and resent.

"Right now, Alan, I really don't care about the company. Besides, this isn't about Logan Publishing. It's about us. You and me. If you can't even trust me to be in your office, why in God's name do you want to marry me?"

His look was one of speechless bewilderment. There was a time it might have amused her. Now, it only fueled her anger.

"You don't trust me at all, do you, Alan? Whenever I come home late from a meeting, or have to stay out of town an extra day...I see your suspicion. And I have *no* idea what I've ever done to make you doubt me. God, what kind of future do we have if you can't even trust me?"

"What's your father going to say?"

"About what? Me leaving the company for a few weeks? He'll understand. Or do you mean me leaving you?"

"You're...you're leaving me?" Alan's mouth hung open and his eyebrows lifted in what Teddy guessed was either disbelief or indignation, but definitely nothing she would qualify as pain.

"Under the circumstances—"

"Teddy, I can explain the accounts...what you saw...and why--"

"For God's sake, this has nothing to do with the accounts!"

Still he looked stunned.

"You don't get it, do you, Alan? It's not just the jealousy and the suspicion. It's your recent obsession with this company. You're becoming my father, for crying out loud. You don't even realize that we've hardly spoken in the last couple of months. Or done anything else together, for that matter." Her words seemed to strike their intended mark— Alan finally let go of her arm and stepped back. "You've changed, Alan. I don't know you anymore."

She'd straightened her suit jacket, and looked him square in the eye.

"I'm leaving. And don't worry about the *company*. I'll speak with my father on my way out." Then she had turned and marched to the door. She hadn't looked back.

"Where will you go, Teddy?"

"I don't know," she'd shouted back over her shoulder.

"How can I reach you?"

"You can't."

"Teddy, wait—"

But she'd kept on walking, and hadn't seen Alan since.

Now, as Teddy steered the Jeep onto the road leading to Sly's cabin, Alan's voice echoed through her mind.

Two years ago, Alan Somerton had breezed into Logan

Publishing and taken the company by storm. Almost instantly, he'd become her father's golden boy, the son he'd always dreamed of. In fact, when Teddy had tried to talk to her father that afternoon, moments after her confrontation in Alan's office, her father wouldn't even listen to her warning that his future son-in-law might be conducting questionable transactions involving the corporate accounts. Her father had waved her away, suggesting that Alan was only being conscientious, and that she was being paranoid. It was then that Teddy realized her father held more faith in Alan than in his own daughter. And it was then that she'd *really* wanted out, *knew* she needed space.

Yes, with his business savvy, Alan had climbed the corporate ladder right on up to vice president, and with his charm, he'd swept Teddy off her feet. But he'd changed.

Teddy pushed back the memories and focused on the road. She took a turn sharper than she probably should have, and was forced to correct the vehicle as it skidded sideways, dangerously close to the right bank. Just beyond that bank of packed snow, Teddy knew the land angled severely downward to sheer cliffs.

Her gloved hands tightened around the steering wheel. She cursed herself for her carelessness. And then she cursed the driver behind her when she saw the headlights glare in her mirror once again.

No, she wasn't being paranoid. She was definitely being followed. And she had less than a mile to lose him.

It had to be Alan, Teddy reasoned as she glanced in the rearview mirror again. He must have hired someone to find her. Exactly why, though, she didn't know. She couldn't believe that Alan was worried enough to try to find her. Nor could she imagine him going to such extremes to save their relationship, unless he was prompted by the unwarranted jealousy that she'd sensed more and more in him lately.

And it certainly wasn't his career. Whether he married the boss's daughter or not, his position with Logan Publishing was secure.

There was more to it than that. Yes, Alan wanted to find her. But why?

Over and over again, Teddy cursed her impulsiveness—she shouldn't have left Denver so rashly, she should have gone back to the office, checked the accounts, found out what Alan had been doing that afternoon. He'd been far too nervous, too anxious about what he *thought* she'd seen. He was up to something—something serious enough to make him send someone after her.

Well, he wasn't going to find her, Teddy resolved as she gripped the wheel and lay her foot heavier on the gas. She would lose the tailing car, backtrack to the cabin and pack her things. She could be out of there, and out of Birdseye, in less than an hour. She could call Sly from the road somewhere, maybe Utah, and apologize for leaving so suddenly.

Then again, maybe she should just give in. If Alan wanted to talk to her that badly, then she should deal with this once and for all.

The other car had lost ground. The headlights grew smaller, but only momentarily. Within seconds, it closed the distance once again.

No! This was not how it was going to happen, Teddy swore to herself. She *would* go back to Denver. She *would* face Alan. But on her own terms. Not with Alan hiring someone to find her as though she was some fugitive.

Teddy gunned the engine. Beyond the reach of her own headlights, she knew where the next intersection lay. A right turn would take her away from the cabin, but she could loop back once she lost the other car. She switched off the dash fan. The only sound now beyond the thrashing wipers was the churning of snow beneath the Jeep's wide tires, and the engine's revving as she pushed it even harder. She fought with the steering as the Jeep dragged through each drift, and she felt the tires grip the cold, packed surface as she turned sharply into the curve.

It was at that moment that Teddy knew she had made a grave error. She'd miscalculated the degree of the turn and the condition of the road. She'd also underestimated the narrow gap between the vehicle and the approaching bank. The second the nose of the Jeep struck the embankment, the steering wheel became useless in her hands.

In nauseating slow motion, she felt the big vehicle ricochet off the packed snow of the bank, let go of the road and begin its death-defying three-hundred-and-sixty-degree spin.

The combined weight and speed of the Jeep propelled it like a missile through the packed bank. There was the groan of metal against hardened snow and ice, and then an ear-splitting shriek that Teddy imagined was the buried guard-rail grinding against the vehicle's belly. Her foot jammed the brake pedal to the floor, but it was useless. The Jeep was airborne, rocketing through the bank and into the night.

In a blink, she saw sheer blackness as the headlights reached out into emptiness. Then there was a brilliant white as the car careened nose-first. In a spine-wrenching jolt, there was blackness again—but this time it was a blackness that seemed to have no end.

DAMN! Mack slammed his open palm against the steering wheel and stared beyond the hood of the Mustang. He'd lost her.

He swore again, turned off the radio and slowed his car.

He'd tried to keep up with her, but she knew these roads, and the Jeep was better suited for such conditions than the Mustang. Not to mention that Teddy Logan was a damned good driver, he thought as he scanned the empty road ahead.

She must have pulled into a lane or a side road, he guessed. She must have killed her lights and was waiting for him to pass. There was no question in his mind that she'd known he was following her. And now Mack could kick himself, because if he didn't find her, she would more than likely double back, pack her things and take off again. And considering the way she had managed to cover her tracks so far, it could be days...even weeks before he found her again.

Sure, he had a general idea where Sly Valeriano's cabin was, but he couldn't be certain. He'd been relying on Teddy to show him the way. He'd thought it was another mile or so up the road he'd just left. But the Jeep had taken a right and he had followed. That was the last he'd seen of the red tail-lights.

He could go back, Mack thought as he geared down. He could turn around and look for the cabin on the other road. Wait for Teddy there. But only *if* he could *find* the cabin. That was a big if.

He scanned the sides of the road, hoping to spot a lane where the Jeep might be parked.

Nothing.

Mack cursed again. This was pointless. If anything, he was only going to become hopelessly lost up here, and he'd hardly come prepared for spending the night in a freezing car in this godforsaken wilderness. He eased his foot off the accelerator as he entered a sharp bend, and instantly saw the skid marks on the snow-packed road. Something had sure taken a spin, but he couldn't tell how recently through the fogged windshield.

And then Mack saw the embankment. Like a gaping mouth, the five-foot-wide opening yawned into the black of night. The guardrail had been exposed, its top brace twisted and curled over. Something had definitely plowed through that bank.

Mack pulled the Mustang to the shoulder and flipped on his hazard lights. From under his seat, he grabbed his flashlight and opened the door.

Frigid wind snatched his breath and sharp snow raked across his exposed skin. Tugging up the collar of his leather bomber jacket, Mack walked past his car toward the opening in the bank. Snow squealed under his boots, but beyond that there was only silence.

He stopped at the opening. The flashlight gleamed off the freshly exposed metal of the guardrail. This was recent, Mack realized as the first wave of dread lurched up from the pit of his stomach. This was very recent.

Panic mobilized him, urging him to the top of the embankment. But even before he got there, even before he swept the beam of his flashlight across the calm white blanket of snow that covered the steep slope, he knew what he was going to find.

The tail end of the black Jeep jutted out, its rear wheels and underbelly exposed, giving it the appearance of some prehistoric beetle attempting to burrow into the frozen earth. The front end was completely buried, the engine dead, the headlights out.

This was his fault, he thought in that instant of heart-stopping panic. If he hadn't been tailing Teddy, this never would have happened. She would not have taken the turn in the road so recklessly in an attempt to lose him, and she would not have lost control of the vehicle.

Mack scrambled over the guardrail, losing his footing twice in his terror. Rock-hard clumps of snow and ice tumbled out from under his boots, and when he pushed off the bank, he swore. He hadn't considered the depth of the snow in these mountains and suddenly he was waist-deep in the stuff.

Mack plowed his way through the heavy snow, slipping on the uneven ground beneath, as he struggled toward the Jeep. Toward Teddy. And by the time he reached the driver's side, he was exhausted. He couldn't tell if his legs were numb from the cold or if his jeans had become so encrusted with snow that he could barely move them. Either way, he had to reach out and use the side of the Jeep for support as he worked his way to the door.

At the driver's window, Mack aimed his flashlight inside, fearing the worst. The bright beam caught Teddy's blond hair. Her face was turned toward him, her right temple nestled against the steering wheel, her eyes closed.

And then Mack saw blood. Just a small trickle along her forehead, but it glistened a brilliant crimson against her pale skin. Mack grappled with the door, wrenching it open and forcing it against the deep snow. The vehicle budged slightly, and for a moment he wondered what lay beyond the nose of the Jeep, praying that the vehicle wasn't teetering on the edge of a snowed-over crevice.

There was no way to tell. And there was no time to check. Yanking off one glove, Mack pressed his fingers against the satiny skin of Teddy's throat. It was as soft as he'd imagined, and just beneath that velvety smoothness he felt the flutter of her pulse under his fingertips.

"Teddy," he whispered urgently, surprised by the sound of her name on his own lips. "Teddy." He called louder this time, as though his voice might penetrate her unconsciousness.

He brushed her hair from her forehead and trained the flashlight there. The cut wasn't severe. A small gash, more of a scrape really, where she'd likely struck her head on the laced edge of the leather-bound steering wheel. The bleeding had already slowed.

Wind and snow howled in through the open door, whipping at Teddy's hair as he gripped her shoulders. He tried to straighten her into the seat, but the cant of the vehicle was too steep. Mack cursed as he fumbled for the seat's lever and in moments he eased her back.

"Teddy." He released the safety harness and said her name again, as though it alone could bring her to consciousness. And for a moment, Mack actually believed that it had worked. He heard her moan, and she shifted in the seat slightly, turning toward him as though she knew he was there to help. But then she was gone again.

"Okay, Teddy," he said. "If that's the way you want it. I got you into this mess, it's only right that I get you out."

He replaced his glove, and stood in the open door for a moment, watching her. After a week of carrying Teddy Logan's photograph...Mack hadn't for a moment expected this.

It was snowing harder. Flakes burst past him and into the Jeep, and Mack watched several settle and melt on Teddy's lips.

Mack glanced back through the blowing snow toward the embankment. The beam of the flashlight revealed his deep path to the road. Only this time, Mack realized, he'd be doing the trek with Teddy Logan in his arms. There was no other way.

He reached in to take the keys from the ignition, and pocketed them along with his flashlight. But even as he reached into the Jeep to get Teddy, Mack prayed that he'd be able to find the cabin, because there was no way he'd make it back down this mountain tonight.

MACK WAS CHILLED to the bone. His jeans were still damp, as was his hair. The heater in the Mustang had done little to take the edge off the cold that gripped him.

Past the thrashing wipers, he saw the glow of the porch light. He'd almost missed it behind the dense underbrush, and now as he pulled into the clearing, he guessed that this had to be Sly Valeriano's cabin. No other vehicle was parked out front, yet it was definitely in use. Fresh-cut wood was stacked on the porch; the walk, although filling in rapidly, had obviously been kept clear; and several low lights had been left on inside.

He turned off the ignition, released his seat belt and looked at Teddy. She was still unconscious.

After he had pulled her from the Jeep a while ago and cradled her easy weight in his arms, Mack had begun his long struggle back to his car. As the wind whipped at the edges of his jacket, Mack had held Teddy even tighter against his chest. Her head had rested on his shoulder and he had felt the warmth of her breath on his neck. It was then that he'd caught the subtle trace of her perfume—something quiet, almost understated, yet undeniably seductive.

He could still smell it now, in the tight confines of the Mustang, and Mack wondered if he could ever encounter that scent again without thinking of Teddy, without remembering the feel of her in his arms, her body warm against his chest.

Giving himself a mental shake, Mack opened the door and let the driving snow and freezing wind force some sense back into him. He was working a case here, he reminded himself as he circled the car. He opened the passenger's door and gazed down at Teddy's perfect features. And when he squatted next to the seat, smelling her perfume again, Mack let out a groan of frustration. Sliding his arms underneath her, he lifted her easily out of the Mustang and shoved the door shut behind him. He would come back for his overnight bag and a fresh pair of jeans once he got her inside.

With Teddy's keys in one hand, Mack shuffled along the snowed-in path and up the steps. In the dim glow of the porch light, he eased Teddy's weight closer against his chest, and flipped through the key ring until he found the one tagged "Sly's." With a sigh of relief, Mack felt the key slide home.

But his relief was short-lived.

The sturdy door opened less than an inch before he heard the low, throaty growl on the other side. Mack didn't need to look inside to know that whatever was behind the door was big.

"Easy, boy. Easy does it," he offered in his most soothing voice, feeling his arms begin to ache.

Another guttural snarl.

"Come on, big guy. Just relax. It's all right. I'm not here to steal anything, okay?" Mack inched the door open, peered into the front hall and saw the malamute poised less than ten feet away.

Well, he'd certainly found the right cabin. Alan Somerton had said Teddy was traveling with her dog, a malamute. And this was certainly the largest malamute Mack had ever laid eyes on. Of course, the thick hairs that bristled up along the animal's back hardly minimized its stature.

With its ears flattened and a deep growl steadily rising from the dog's broad chest, the animal was definitely a force to be reckoned with. Still, he had to get Teddy inside.

Mack took one tentative step into the cabin's warmth. Instantly, the dog's lips curled back to reveal long, dangerous canines.

"Come on, boy. Take it easy. Good boy. Go lie down. Sit. Stay. Fetch."

The dog refused to budge.

"Damn!" Mack dared to tear his gaze from the dog to the woman in his arms. "Listen to me, Teddy Logan. If you're anywhere *near* regaining consciousness here, well, this might be a pretty good time, you know?" But her eyes remained closed. Behind him, the wind howled, sweeping great gusts of snow in through the front door and down the hallway.

"Okay, listen up, pooch. Here's the thing." He took another step into the cabin and slowly eased the door shut behind him with one boot. "Now, you just relax, and once I get a second, I'll find you a biscuit or something. Deal?"

The malamute held its ground, but had stopped growling.

"I'm going to pretend like you're not even here, okay? And maybe you can do the same. What do you say?"

The hair on the dog's back seemed to settle.

Beyond the animal, the cabin lay in a warm yellow glow— rather inviting when compared to the malamute that barred his path. To the right was a cozy living room dominated by a massive flagstone fireplace, its furniture rustic yet functional, and to the left lay a small but modern kitchen. It was down the hall, past the dog, that Mack saw the single bedroom.

Mack took a step toward the dog. "All right, pooch. This is it. Either you let me past, or I swear to God, I'm going to have to—"

But the dog made its move first. In one heart-stopping lunge it was at Mack's side—but not to bite him, Mack realized with a hot shudder of relief as the animal sniffed Teddy's boots and started wagging its tail.

"All right then. That's more like it. Friends?"

The dog cocked its white face and gazed up at him, and Mack could have sworn it actually understood that he was here to help.

When he carried Teddy down the hall, the dog trotted calmly at his side, and when Mack pushed open the bedroom door, the animal was one step ahead of him.

Light spilled into the room from the hallway behind him; enough for Mack to find the bed. He lowered Teddy onto it, but before he drew back, Mack felt her breath brush across his cheek. In that second, he thought he'd heard her whisper something.

He hovered close to her, his face only inches from hers, their breath mingling. Had she said something? Or had it been his own pounding heart that he'd heard?

Without moving from his position over her, Mack reached to the bedside lamp. "Teddy?" When he looked down at her again, the soft light played across her delicate features—her high cheekbones, her straight, perfect nose and that strong, almost defiant jawline. Gently he brushed several blond wisps of hair from her forehead, marveling at its silkiness. The small gash had stopped bleeding. He could tend to it later, he decided, hoping there was a first-aid kit somewhere in the cabin.

But first, he had to get her warm. She'd had her coat open in the Jeep, and when he'd carried her through the storm, she'd been bombarded with as much snow as he had. Both the fleece lining of her coat and her clothes were damp.

He'd have to undress her. There was no way around it.

Standing back from the bed, Mack cast a quick glance at the malamute. The massive dog filled the doorway, watching him, as though waiting to see what he would do next.

"I tell you what, old boy—" Mack turned to Teddy again as he spoke to the animal "—I won't look if you don't."

He started with her boots, unlacing them and dropping

each to the floor with a loud thud. Then her gloves and scarf. When he brushed open her Gore-Tex coat, he gingerly drew each arm from the sleeves before lifting her slightly to remove the coat.

She moaned once, but didn't wake. Tossing the coat onto a nearby chair, Mack paused when he looked at her. "Then again," he said to the dog, "it's probably nothing *you* haven't already seen, huh? Lucky fella."

Beneath the thin, clinging fabric of the low-cut top she wore, every line and angle, every seductive curve was enticingly revealed, shifting with each quiet breath—the slender waist, the hollow of her stomach, the soft swell of her breasts...all so tantalizing.

Mack groaned inwardly. This was definitely *not* what he'd had in mind when he'd decided to make contact with Teddy Logan.

"Teddy?" He sat down on the edge of the bed and touched his hand to the cool skin of her cheek. "Teddy?" he whispered again, wishing that she'd regain consciousness now, yet not knowing what he'd say if she actually did. Somehow, hovering over her as she lay in bed hardly seemed an appropriate introduction. But then, neither did undressing her.

Mack took in a deep breath and lowered his hand from Teddy's cheek to her shoulder. Her clothes were definitely damp from the snow. He had to get her out of them and under the covers.

The cabin had fallen into an almost unearthly silence. The only sound was Teddy's low breathing. Mack wondered if he could actually hear her heartbeat over his own as his hand inched toward the row of silver buttons along the front of her top.

His breath locked in his throat as he carefully unsnapped one button after the next. And with each one, more and more lace was revealed--elegant black lace flowers against pale, almost luminous skin. He tugged the ends of her top from the waist of her jeans and delicately brushed back the sides. Shadows contoured each soft curve. The low lamplight kissed every gently rounded form, as though inviting him to touch, to trail his fingers along those enticing planes and angles, and to feel the satiny radiance of her skin. And for a second, Mack could almost imagine the searing tingle that would make his heart stop if he were to feel the caress of that skin against his own.

Mack heard another groan. But this time it was his own. He exhaled a long sigh of frustration. This was insane. Absolutely insane! He shouldn't do this. Couldn't!

He knew better. He'd learned firsthand how personal involvement in a case only led to disaster. It had been two years ago, working on the Denver Narcotics Unit, an entire summer of undercover...deep cover. Too deep, as it turned out. To this day, Mack could still hear the gunshot ricochet through his memory. Blake—his partner on the force, the man he'd worked with for five years, his best friend—had taken the bullets. And all because of a woman. All because Mack had let himself get too involved, *personally* involved. Blake survived, but Mack knew it should have been *him* who'd paid for his mistakes, not Blake. *He* was the one who had screwed up the assignment, who had lost his focus.

Working for himself as a private investigator meant that no one relied on him now. If he screwed up, *he* took the consequences. No one else. Even so, he knew better...

"Alan?"

This time Mack was certain he'd heard Teddy whisper. He drew his gaze to her face. Her eyebrows knitted together, and her forehead tightened briefly, as though she'd found herself in some disquieting dream. She shook her head once, and murmured again. "Alan?"

"I gotta be nuts," Mack whispered to himself as he slipped Teddy's top from her bare shoulders and started turning down the covers.

He shook his head. How much crazier could it get? Here he was in a remote mountain cabin in the middle of the night, undressing and fantasizing about the woman he'd been hired to find, while *she* was dreaming of her fiancé.

3

SHE WAS BACK at the estate—her father's house—in the west wing, where she had lived for the past three years. She was carrying a suitcase and a shoulder bag down the wide curving staircase to the front hall. Bogie was at the door, his tail fanning the air.

She wasn't sure where she was going. Only that she had to get away—from the office, from Denver, but especially from Alan. When her father refused to heed her warnings, she'd made up some story about visiting a sick friend out of town. She didn't want him worrying, but more than that, she didn't want her father meddling in her personal life, trying to persuade her to stay and work things out with Alan.

Then she was out the door. She piled the bags along with Bogie in the back of the Jeep, and headed out. A thick fog lay low across the oak-lined driveway, even though it was January. Then suddenly, Alan came out of nowhere. He'd stepped out of a swirl of luminescent fog and onto the driveway.

He was wearing the same gray Armani suit he'd worn back at the office. And he had the same dark fury in his eyes.

"You can't go, Teddy," she heard him shout. "I won't let you."

He brought his hands up, gesturing for her to stop. Her foot lunged for the brakes, but found nothing. Only air. And the Jeep careened forward, barreling toward him. She called out. Screaming for Alan to move.

Then there was a voice—strangely familiar. It whispered her name. Somehow she knew the voice was not a part of this dream. And it *was* a dream. She knew that, because even as the voice called her a second time, the Jeep hurtled toward the apparition of Alan and then seemed to pass directly through him as though he were an extension of the fog itself.

"Teddy?"

"Alan," she gasped. "Alan!"

"Teddy, can you hear me?"

There was a hand on her shoulder, firm and warm. No, this was not part of her dream.

She opened her eyes, squinting against the glare of sunshine. "Alan?" She searched for him in the harsh light.

"Uh, no. It's not Alan." She couldn't place the soothing voice, and yet Teddy felt as though she should know it.

She blinked, adjusting to the light until she could see the man hovering over her.

Teddy jerked away from the stranger as though the hand on her shoulder was a hot iron. Her own startled gasp cut through the room. She was definitely awake now. She gripped the edge of the covers and pulled them tighter around her.

"Who the hell are you?"

"It's all right. Just relax," he assured her, his voice so smooth and calm, it alone should have convinced her that she had nothing to fear from this man. He backed off, stepping away from the bed. "My name's Mack Carlino."

The hand he extended was wide, with large, square knuckles and the memory of a deep summer tan. When Teddy took it cautiously in hers, the strength of his grip did not surprise her. What *did* surprise her, was how comfortably her hand lingered in his, much longer than any introduction should warrant.

"You...you were in the bar," she said eventually, slipping her hand from his. She drew herself up against the headboard and pulled the covers to her chin. "I saw you in the bar. Last night."

Mack Carlino nodded.

She should have recognized him the second she'd opened her eyes. How could she forget that dark, penetrating gaze and the jet-black hair, those broad shoulders and the obviously toned physique that moved just beneath the rumpled shirt and jeans? Up close, Teddy realized that she hadn't given the man half the credit he'd deserved for his good looks. From across the dingy bar, she hadn't seen the finer definition of his chiseled features, the square jaw, or the small cleft in his strong chin. Last night she'd considered him undeniably handsome, but standing over her now, in the light of day, Mack Carlino was nothing less than stunning. Even if he was in need of a shave.

"You were at the bar," she repeated as though it might help her recall how she came to be in her bed this morning with this stranger in her room.

"Do you remember what happened last night?" His voice—so deeply seductive—seemed to reach out and wrap itself around her like a lover's tender embrace.

Teddy released the breath she'd been holding, trying to shake the arousing illusions that whispered behind her mind's eye. "Yes." She nodded. "An accident. I went off the road, didn't I?"

Carlino took another step back from the bed, and slid his hands into the pockets of his faded jeans as he regarded her with those mesmerizing dark eyes of his. "Yes, you did. You missed a turn and took your Jeep through a snowbank."

Teddy lifted a hand to the throbbing tenderness along her forehead and felt the dressing.

"You were damned lucky you didn't go nose-first down the mountainside."

And then it all came back to her—saying good-night to Sly, leaving the bar, seeing the headlights in her rearview mirror. What were the chances of anyone else being up on that road at that time of night?

"You were following me," she said, hearing accusation sharpen her words. Thoughts of Alan and the suspicions that had caused her to swerve off the road flared anew.

"Well, I wasn't *exactly* following you," he told her.

"So what are you saying? You just happened to be going the same way? There's nothing up on this side of the mountain except a few cabins, Mr. Carlino."

"Please, call me Mack. And actually, I took a wrong turn."

"A 'wrong turn.'" Teddy could not have summoned up more sarcasm if she'd tried.

"Yes, a wrong turn. It's not as if these roads are well marked. When I saw your taillights, I tried to catch up with you, hoping to ask directions."

"So why didn't you flash your lights or something? To get my attention?"

"And would you have stopped in the middle of the night?" He tilted his head, raising his eyebrows inquisitively as the corners of his lips curled slightly.

Teddy studied him for a long moment, taking in those handsome features and that charming half smile of his. A man this good-looking...it didn't seem possible he could lie.

"Wait a second, how did you even know this was my cabin?"

Under other circumstances, the smile he gave her with a slight head shake might have melted her heart. But right now, Teddy could see very little beyond her cold suspicion.

"You know, for a woman who's just been whacked on the head, you sure do ask a lot of questions, Ms. Logan."

"You...you know my name?"

"I'm sorry," he said, his voice calm and assured as he started to pace. "I checked your wallet. I was hoping to find a local address, and when I didn't, I figured you were staying in one of these rental cabins up here. I drove around a bit, saw the lights and knocked on the door. When I didn't get an answer, I figured I may as well try your keys." He shrugged. "I got lucky. By the way, that's some guard dog you've got there. I almost didn't make it past the front door."

He must have seen the trace of worry in her face, because he added, "He's all right. He's in the other room."

Maybe it was the blow to the head, Teddy reasoned. She should be more shocked, more alarmed, at waking up to find a man in her bedroom. And yet, she wasn't. For some reason that she couldn't put her finger on, she wasn't afraid of Mack Carlino.

He'd crossed the bedroom to one of the large northeast windows and was staring out at the sun-drenched snow. With his back turned, Teddy studied him from behind—his broad shoulders, the gradual taper of his torso to that narrow waist, and then his tight denim-hugged buttocks.

Ashamed at her blatant staring, Teddy dragged her gaze away. It was then that she noticed the rocking chair. Normally the old rocker with the sheepskin throw sat in the corner of the room, but now it was pulled up alongside the bed. And over the back was draped the wool blanket from the living room.

He'd kept a vigil over her. Mack Carlino had sat next to her bed and watched her through the night. And even though this knowledge should have caused a certain uneasiness, Teddy found herself touched by his gracious concern.

She looked at him again, his back still partially turned. The morning sunlight softened the strong lines of his profile and she wondered why she should think of angels—guardian angels.

Who was Mack Carlino? And what had brought him to her? Was it coincidence? Or were her suspicions last night something she should be heeding this morning?

Teddy wasn't sure what she was about to ask him, but when he turned his dark gaze onto her, the capability of speech seemed to have left her. She could only stare into his seductively mysterious eyes, and wonder.

"IT'S STOPPED SNOWING," Mack told her, needing to fill the sudden silence. It seemed that Teddy Logan didn't know *what* to say to him, he thought as he held her gaze. "The plows should probably be getting through in the next hour or so, I'd imagine."

Still, she was silent.

"I think you should probably see someone. A doctor, I mean." He slid his hands into his pockets and crossed the room to the foot of the heavy pine queen-size bed. "That's quite a bump you've got."

She nodded.

"Once the roads are cleared, I'll drive you into Birdseye, or the nearest hospital. Get you looked at."

She nodded again.

"I gotta say, though, Teddy, the way your Jeep went off the road like that, you're one lucky woman."

Instantly, her face darkened. Confusion tightened her soft features.

"What is it?" he asked.

"You...you called me Teddy."

Damn! He hadn't even realized her name had slipped out. Why on *earth* was he so nervous?

Mack shrugged, grappling for a quick recovery. "Like I said, I checked your wallet."

"But my ID doesn't—"

"Theodora. I know." He was floundering now. *Get a grip!* he scolded himself. What was wrong with him? He never fumbled with this kind of stuff. Undercover, he'd been one of the squad's best when he'd still been on the force. And now, confronted by a beautiful woman, he was an utter basket case.

"The men at the bar—I heard them call you Teddy. I just figured..." He shrugged, hoping he sounded convincing. "I'm sorry, I shouldn't have presumed familiarity."

She studied him. Skepticism clouded her cool blue-gray eyes for a brief moment, then diminished. "No, you're right," she said. "I mean, it's okay. My friends call me Teddy."

She gave him a smile, and he was struck by how it lit up her eyes. She didn't look as pale as she had late last night, Mack decided. In fact, seeing her propped up by the pillows against the headboard, Mack could almost forget that she could have quite easily lost her life along that dark, treacherous road. And that he would have been responsible.

"So, Mr. Carlino—"

"Mack," he corrected her.

Her smile, although still cautious, quieted his darker thoughts.

"Mack, then," she said. The sound of his name on her lips, spoken in that silken voice, sent an unexpected wave of heat coursing through him. "I suppose I'm eternally indebted to you...for saving my life."

"No. Not at all. It was luck. If it hadn't been me, someone else would have dragged you out of that Jeep."

She nodded thoughtfully, still eyeing him warily.

"Can I ask what it is you do for a living? And what's

brought you to Birdseye? Are you renting a cabin, as well? Or are you just passing through?"

"Whoa." He held up his hand, and couldn't resist a quiet chuckle. "Why don't we play Sixty Questions over coffee? I don't know about you, but I need caffeine. Here—" He reached for the terry robe from the back of the door and draped it over the end of the bed. "I'll start the coffee. Why don't you get dressed?"

Teddy's smile dissolved. With the covers still pulled to her chin, she didn't move, but judging by the flush that instantly flared across her cheeks, Mack guessed that she hadn't realized until now that she was almost naked. And there certainly was no one else around who might have undressed her.

For a moment, Mack relished the sudden color to her cheeks, knowing that he was the one who'd caused it. But simply remembering the tantalizing task of undressing Teddy made him wish he could forget it. It was precisely those memories that made looking at her now so difficult. And as he felt another hot swell stir deep inside of him, Mack was grateful for the bed's footboard that separated him from Teddy. At least she wouldn't be able to see the effect she was having on him, he thought as he felt the restriction of heavy denim.

"Just shout if you need a hand," he said at last, unable to think of anything else to say before he turned and left the room.

Dammit! What was *wrong* with him? Mack stopped in the middle of the hallway and glanced back at the closed bedroom door. Sure, he'd always been a bit of a ladies' man, especially when he'd been a cop. He'd had his share of relationships—some casual, some long-term. But never...*never* had a woman affected him to the extent Teddy Logan did.

Hell, a simple tilt of her head seemed enough to knot his stomach and set his groin on fire.

"Get a grip, Carlino," he whispered to himself, shaking his head and walking to the kitchen.

Ten minutes later the coffee machine on the corner of the porcelain-tiled counter hissed to life. And still, Mack couldn't let go of the images of last night, the electrifying tingle of Teddy's skin under his fingertips as he'd undressed her, the warmth of her breath against his wrist as he'd cleaned and dressed the cut on her forehead, and finally, the sound of her breathing and her quiet moans through the night.

Mack leaned back against the counter and crossed his arms over his chest. He let out a long breath, as though he could exhale his tension. And then he glanced at the phone mounted on the kitchen wall.

He had to call Denver. There was no other way. He couldn't go through with this. It no longer mattered that he know Teddy's side of the story. He needed to get away from her. He was insane to have let things go this far. Past experience should have been enough to warn him not to get personally involved, and here he was standing in her kitchen.

Mack reached for the phone. Yes. He would call Alan Somerton, tell him he'd accomplished his assignment, give him the address and go home to Denver to collect the rest of his fee. And soon the intense longing that stirred deep inside of him whenever Teddy turned that smoky gray-eyed gaze on him would be a distant memory.

He lifted the receiver to his ear, but in that same second, the bedroom door opened behind him.

Mack spun around in time to meet Teddy's questioning stare.

"WHO WERE YOU PHONING?" Teddy asked as she came down the hall to the kitchen with Bogie at her side.

Mack had hung up the receiver quickly when she'd stepped out of the bedroom only seconds ago. Even now, he seemed unnecessarily nervous. "No one," he said. "I was checking the lines. The phone was dead last night. I figured the storm must have taken the lines down."

"Is it working now?"

"Seems to be."

Teddy stood within arm's reach of him, holding his dark stare. She could get lost in that gaze, she realized. His eyes seemed to caress her rather than look at her.

"Good," she said finally, needing to break the silence. "Then I can call someone about my Jeep."

Mack nodded, and she was about to brush past him when she felt the kitchen start to spin and her knees go weak. Teddy didn't even realize she had faltered until Mack caught her. In a flash he was at her side, his strong arms wrapping tightly around her waist. He pulled her to him, and she felt the power of his body press against hers for that brief moment before she was able to right herself. Her hand found his forearm; his shirtsleeve was rolled up and beneath the warm skin Teddy felt the play of iron-hard muscles.

But even when Teddy had regained her balance, Mack didn't release her entirely. He held her steady, both hands planted firmly on her hips as though not trusting her to stand without help. When he moved around in front of her, Teddy was surprised at the degree of concern that marked his features.

"I'm fine," she tried to assure him. But he didn't look convinced. "Really, Mack," she added with a forced smile. "I'm all right."

"Sure you are," he said, shaking his head. "You're totally

fine, and that's why you're almost passing out on me." He
ushered her to one of the kitchen chairs. "I am definitely getting you to a hospital this morning."

"It was just a dizzy spell, Mack. It hardly warrants a trip
to the hospital." But the truth was, there was no way Teddy
was getting anywhere near a doctor. If she let Mack take her
to the hospital in Craig, there would be forms to fill out, and
forms meant a paper trail...and Alan.

She allowed Mack to ease her into the chair and then
watched him rummage through the refrigerator.

"I'm not going to hear any argument, Teddy. You've had
a blow to the head. Heck, if it wasn't for the storm last night,
you would have been waking up in a hospital bed this
morning. You need to get checked out. End of argument."

Teddy bit back her words. Under other circumstances,
she would have taken a stand. With a few select words, she
would have put the authoritative Mack Carlino in his
place...and out of hers. But whether it was the blow to her
head, or the magnetic charm that lay just beneath Mack's
overbearing attitude, Teddy found herself incapable of ob-
jection.

She closed her eyes and rubbed her temples, trying to
ease the flaring headache. When she opened her eyes again,
Mack was busy at the counter. Teddy glanced at the phone.
He hadn't just been checking it. She'd seen the apprehension in his face when she'd stepped out of the bedroom—
like a child caught with his hand in the cookie jar.

Who was Mack Carlino? And what right did she have to
be suspicious of him? Especially after what he'd done for
her last night—bringing her here, spending the night in the
chair next to her bed instead of taking the couch, watching
over her. She owed him her life.

Her gaze, almost involuntarily, returned to Mack. He had
his back to her as he poured orange juice and put bread into

the toaster. She watched his strong hands, beautiful hands. The same hands that had undressed her, Teddy thought, feeling another flush warm her cheeks as she imagined him doing so. What had he taken off first? How long had he stood there, watching her? How had he touched her? Had he been indifferent? Or had he derived a certain pleasure from undressing her? Had he practiced restraint when leaving her with her bra and panties?

Mack turned, as though aware of her thoughts. And the intimate smile that touched his lips seemed to answer Teddy's question. Reflexively, she lifted a hand to the top of her shirt and drew the edges tighter across her throat.

"Would you like some juice?"

She nodded.

"So where *is* the nearest hospital around here anyway?" he asked, handing her the glass.

"I would guess Craig. It's at least an hour's drive. But honestly, there's no need. I'm fine."

He ignored her protest, and perched himself on the corner of the table next to her. She felt the heat of his body then, drawing closer, sending a sudden, almost electric warmth through her, and for a moment Teddy had no idea what he intended to do. She started to draw away, until he caught her chin in his hand and tilted her head.

"It's all right, Teddy." She saw his quick smile and didn't doubt that he sensed her tension. "I don't bite."

With his other hand he reached for the bandage on her forehead. She tried to relax. Strong fingers carefully peeled back the adhesive, and he inspected the gash. He said nothing, and then, with a tenderness she'd never imagined from a man, Mack replaced the gauze.

He was so close to her now, his thigh touching her arm, his strong fingers still holding her chin. Teddy felt the heat of his breath whisper across her lips.

Snap out of it, she told herself as she bit her lower lip. Mack Carlino was a stranger, for God's sake. She knew absolutely nothing about the man. He meant nothing to her.

Why, then, should his every touch feel so seductive? Why did her heart race, and why on earth should she feel such arousal when he was doing no more than checking her bandage? And in that instant, Teddy couldn't remember if Alan had ever made her feel this way.

"Who *are* you, Mack Carlino?" she asked in a whisper so soft she wondered if he'd even heard her. But when she looked up and met Mack's dark gaze, there was little doubt that he had.

4

IT COULD HAVE BEEN the faint trace of her now-familiar perfume, or the way those silver eyes gazed up into his, or maybe even the way her lips lingered on the last syllable of his name, but Mack had an overwhelming urge to kiss Teddy at that moment. With her face tilted toward his, it would have been so easy to close the few inches between them and taste her lips. To end the fantasizing, to find out once and for all if they were as supple and sweet as he imagined them to be.

Mack withdrew his hand and shifted from the corner of the table. He needed space. Crossing to the kitchen counter, he turned his attention to the coffee machine. Caffeine. That's what he needed. A bit of caffeine would bring him to his senses.

"You're not from around here, are you, Mack?"

"No," he answered quickly, keeping his attention on the task of pouring coffee.

"You're just passing through then?"

"That's right. Leaving Denver." Still, he kept his back to Teddy, afraid that if he met her gaze—the gaze of the woman whom he'd undressed only hours ago and spent most of his night fantasizing about—he would crack.

"So where are you headed?"

"Idaho. Boise, actually," he lied.

"And what's in Boise?"

"My brother."

When he turned, he looked at her through a thin veil of steam from his mug. She drew her hair over one shoulder, and he watched the sunshine glimmer off its golden highlights. He fought to remain calm, to keep his head.

Last night, as he'd sat next to her bed, he'd pieced together a story. He'd rehearsed exactly what he'd tell Teddy, and yet, face-to-face with her now, it took everything he had just to form a single, coherent sentence.

"A brother?" The calm determination that turned up the corners of her mouth made it clear that Teddy was not about to be deceived so easily. He'd have to be careful.

"Yes. My brother has a carpentry business. He called me the other week to ask if I'd help out. I guess business is good."

"So is that who you were calling?"

"Pardon me?"

"When you were on the phone."

"No, I was only checking the lines. But yes, I should probably give him a call and let him know I've gotten waylaid."

"He's expecting you, then?"

"Not exactly. I told him he'd see me when I got there. I thought I'd take the scenic route." He nodded out the window. "It's a little more scenic than I'd bargained for, though."

Mack leaned back against the counter, cradling his cup between his hands, and waited as Teddy studied him openly. He wondered if she was buying any of his story. No doubt her suspicions had been on alert from the moment she'd caught the Mustang's headlights in her rearview mirror. And he couldn't blame her for her skepticism. Waking up to find a complete stranger in her bedroom—it was a wonder she was speaking with him at all.

At last she pulled her gaze from his and looked momentarily to the malamute sitting by her side, a silent sentinel.

"So, Mack Carlino, what is it you do for a living then? Somehow I just don't have you pegged for a carpenter like your brother in Boise, Idaho."

He shared her quick, quietly knowing smile. "I could ask the same of you, Teddy Logan. You don't exactly strike me as the type to be bartending in a town like Birdseye. And no offense, but this cabin...it's not really you, if you know what I mean." He gestured to the rustic decor of the living room behind him.

"Yes, well, you're very perceptive, Mack. This cabin isn't mine. I'm renting. But I asked you first. What is it you do for a living?"

Mack looked out the window again, to where his car sat in the driveway under a good foot of snow. Everything was there, in that car, including his gun. To someone as intuitive as Teddy, it was easy evidence of his real life back in Denver. There would be no way of hiding it from her, and no point in attempting to convince her that he was anything but what he was—a former cop. If nothing else, his years of undercover work had taught him that the surest way to maintain a cover was to stick close to the truth. After all, a web, even of one's own lies, was still a web.

"How much do you want to bet that I can guess your profession?" she asked before he could answer. It was the slight tilt of her head and the openness of her smile that displayed her challenge, and Mack allowed himself to become momentarily lost in her honest humor. "Come on. Three tries. I bet I can guess."

"And what makes you so sure?"

"It's a game I used to play while tending bar in my college days. I think I've still got the knack."

"Three guesses, hmm? And what are the stakes?"

She drew her feet up onto the edge of the chair, circling her knees with her arms, and seemed to contemplate her options for a moment. But her eyes never left his. Even when she finally spoke, her gaze was fixed with such determination that Mack found himself shifting uneasily.

"If I can guess your profession," she challenged, "you agree not to drag me to some stuffy doctor's office or a crowded emergency room in Craig."

"And if you can't guess, we're leaving right after I finish this coffee. Deal?" He tipped his cup at her and she nodded as though sealing the contract.

"Deal."

"All right, then. Give it your best shot."

The scrutiny with which she studied him was enough to make Mack regret his wager. Those cool gray eyes seemed to bore right into him, holding his gaze as though she could reach into his mind and snatch her answers directly. Only once did her gaze stray, and she looked to where her hand rested on the malamute's broad head, as though the dog might somehow offer a clue.

And then a quick and assured light flickered into her eyes, a glimmer of laughter that brought a smile to his lips even as he watched her.

"I've got it."

"You have, have you?"

"You play for the Denver Broncos."

Mack let out a short laugh and shook his head. "Strike one. But I suppose I'm flattered that you think so. Next guess."

"All right, then. Let's see. How about...small-dog trainer?"

Her warm laughter rippled through the silence of the cabin, above his own then, and Mack found himself captivated by its sound.

"Well, now I *know* you're only guessing," he said.

"You're grasping at straws, Teddy. I think I'll get your coat."

"Not so fast. I have three guesses."

"Okay, number three."

"All right. Here goes. Number three. I'm willing to bet a trip to the doctor's that you, Mack Carlino, are a cop."

There was no laughter this time, even though a smile still curved Teddy's lips and a healthy flush colored her once-paled complexion.

How could she have possibly guessed? In the short time she'd known him, what had given him away? Even more astonishing than her final guess was the assuredness with which Teddy had delivered it. She couldn't have been more confident had he been standing there with his police revolver strapped to his side and a pair of cuffs dangling off the back of his belt.

"I'm right, aren't I?"

From over the rim of his mug, Mack held her stare for a long moment before tilting the cup back and finishing his coffee. He set the empty mug on the counter. "Come on, we're going to find you a doctor."

"I'm wrong?" Her disbelief cut through the silence of the cabin, and he heard her chair scrape back against the floorboards even as he started to the door for her coat.

"Mack," she called after him. "Are you saying I'm wrong?"

He stopped in the hall and turned to look at her. "Yes, you're wrong. Now, can we go? I really think you need to see a doctor, Teddy." He gave her a smile, but she was quite obviously dissatisfied with his apparent dismissal of their game.

"You're telling me you're not a cop?"

"That's what I'm saying. I am not a cop. I *used* to be a cop, but not anymore."

"So I was right."

"Only partly." He reached for her coat. "I told you already—I'm a carpenter."

"Not till you get to Boise." She planted her hands on her hips and smiled again, as though challenging him to fulfill their bargain.

"Come on, let's go." He held up her coat for her, but Teddy wouldn't budge.

"So are you at least going to tell me why you gave up police work?"

"Let's just say I'm on an indefinite leave," he responded, thinking of his gun tucked under the driver's seat of the Mustang, and knowing that Teddy would likely question it if he didn't pretend to be a cop on leave.

"And you're not going to tell me why?"

"That's a long story. Besides, what about you?"

"What about me?"

"Oh, come on, a woman like you, up here, in the middle of nowhere—"

"Tending bar in a backwoods mountain town like Birdseye, you mean?"

"Yeah."

"Well, Mack Carlino—" there was defiance in her voice "—I guess I could say that's an equally long story."

He nodded, admiring her alacrity. "Fair enough."

But even if Mack had wished to pursue the subject further, he wouldn't have been able to. The malamute barged its way past him to the front door seconds before either of them heard the four-wheel drive's engine.

There was the muted thud of footsteps across the porch, and then the dog let out one deep howl at the sound of the knock.

Mack unlatched the door and swung it open to a gust of

frigid air. He recognized the man on the porch, the snowy-haired proprietor of the bar—Sly Valeriano.

"Good morning, sir," Mack offered, squinting at the brilliance of the sun on freshly fallen snow.

"Who are you?"

"Mack Carlino." He extended his hand but the gesture was not reciprocated.

"Where's Teddy?" the man demanded, suspicion creasing his already wrinkled expression.

"She's—"

"I'm here, Sly," Teddy called out, and when Mack turned to look at her, he realized that she hadn't moved from the kitchen doorway. Her complexion had paled again, and he could see that she leaned heavily against the jamb for support. "I'm all right," she said, but she hardly looked it.

Sly Valeriano pushed past Mack into the front hall and started toward Teddy. One gloved hand patted the malamute's head as it followed him.

"We found your Jeep. Graham's towing it out right now. What the hell happened?"

Teddy shrugged, sharing a quick glance with Mack before looking back to the old man. "I guess I kind of missed a curve in the road last night. I don't remember what happened exactly, but luckily Mack here found me. I'm fine though, Sly. Really. In fact, I'm glad you're here. Maybe you can convince Mack that I don't need to be dragged all the way to Craig to see some doctor."

"No." He shook his white-haired head. "No, I agree. There's no sense in driving all the way out to Craig."

"See?" The smile she gave Mack then was one of pure, almost childlike triumph.

But her smile faded just as quickly as it had come when Sly replied; "You can see Doc Wharton in town. He's better 'n any Craig doctor anyhow."

It was Mack's turn to retaliate with a conquering smile.

"Are you heading out now?" Sly directed his question to Mack this time.

"Shortly."

"Then I'll let Doc Wharton know you're on your way so he doesn't close up before you get there. He doesn't put in many hours on Wednesdays. You'll find him at the south end of the main street. Can't miss the place."

"Thank you," Mack said.

But the look that Sly shot him held no more trust than the man's first glance. He turned back to Teddy, his concern for her more than apparent as he removed his glove and took her hand in his.

"You're sure you're all right, Teddy?"

"I'm fine, Sly. Thanks."

Two weeks Teddy had been in Birdseye and she'd already managed to win her way into the hearts of the locals. Then again, Mack was hardly surprised. After all, *he* had known her less than twelve hours and already the mere sound of her laughter affected him in a way that he didn't want to think about.

"Listen, Teddy," Sly continued, "I don't want you coming to work the bar if you don't feel up to it. In fact, I insist that you take a couple days off. And if you have a chance later, after seeing Doc Wharton, why don't you stop in and pick up your pay."

Teddy nodded. Her face was almost white now, and Mack didn't doubt that without the support of the doorjamb, she would not be standing. Casually, he crossed the hall to stand next to her. The act brought yet another suspicious glower from Sly.

"Right, then," the old man said at last, "I'll see you in town, Teddy. And I'll be sure that Graham looks at your Jeep first thing. You guys had better leave soon though, 'fore the snow picks up again. This blizzard hasn't played itself out yet."

"Thanks, Sly," Teddy said as he headed out the door. "I'll stop by later."

It wasn't until the muted rumble of Sly's four-wheel drive had faded that Mack finally turned to Teddy.

"Are you ready?" he asked.

She let out an exasperated sigh. "Mack, I honestly—"

"Look, Teddy, if it's the last thing I do in Birdseye, I'm going to see to it that you're all right."

He held up her coat once again, and caught a flicker of defeat in her eyes. It was a look that he suspected rarely crossed Teddy Logan's face, and she seemed almost uncomfortable with the idea that he'd successfully gained the upper hand in this situation.

And as he helped her with her coat, Mack wondered if Teddy believed his story, or if she saw right through him and recognized that he had ulterior motives for staying in Birdseye— motives that went far beyond the parameters of his assignment.

ALAN SOMERTON paced the floor-to-ceiling windows of his office and looked out over the flat, cold expanse of the Denver skyline. He hated Denver.

Thirty miles west, the dim silhouette of the Front Range hung in the gray sky. He thought of Teddy, out there...somewhere. She knew too much. Had seen too much. He was sure of it. Where the hell was she? And why hadn't he heard from Mack Carlino yet?

Maybe he should have hired someone else. After all, it wasn't just his position with Logan Publishing that was at stake now. Embezzlement...that was a criminal offense.

Casting a glance at his desk, his eye caught the photograph next to his computer. Teddy's smile shone back, as radiant as the golden hair that framed her features. But Alan saw little beauty in that smile this morning. There was a time when the sight of it had warmed his heart, when he could close his eyes and remember her smell and her laughter, when he could have imagined a future with Teddy. But now all he saw in that tarnishing brass frame was his ruin.

TEDDY HAD INITIALLY had her doubts about the Mustang getting them down the mountain, even though the plows had been through. But Mack had proven himself a superior driver, and although they hadn't made it to Birdseye in record time, they'd gotten there without incident.

Now Mack slowed the car as they cruised toward the south end of the main street, searching for Doc Wharton's office. Teddy snatched another glance at Mack as he concentrated on the road. She'd done a lot of that during the drive down—watching him, studying his strong, unshaven profile, admiring his wide hands around the wheel, and then imagining where those hands had been last night.

Her imagination, combined with the lingering trace of Mack's after-shave and a definite underlying male scent, made the closeness of the Mustang's interior seem almost intimate. But what surprised Teddy even more was that she didn't feel uncomfortable in that intimacy. Nor was she bothered by Mack's authoritative nature. In fact, she'd found herself rather charmed by his display of masculine chivalry. His determination to look after her was a quality she couldn't remember ever seeing in Alan.

Casting another scrupulous glance over the interior of the cluttered car, Teddy again eyed the tan strap of the partially hidden gun holster on the floor. When Mack had first opened the passenger door for her at the cabin, she'd watched him swiftly push aside a duffel bag and several magazines. But, in spite of his efforts to conceal it, the leather holster tucked under the driver's seat hadn't escaped Teddy's notice. He was a cop on leave; an "indefinite leave," he'd told her. Of course he'd have his weapon, she convinced herself and directed her attention to the rest of the car's contents.

With only two small bags in the back seat, it didn't appear as though Mack was headed anywhere for very long, let alone all the way to Idaho to join his brother in some carpentry business. She tried to give him the benefit of the doubt, wishing that she wasn't so damned suspicious until she saw the dog-eared business card on the dash, tucked in amongst what appeared to be receipts and a few parking tickets. When she was certain that Mack's concentration was on the road, she'd taken a closer look at the card: Ryan Carlino, Renovations and Fine Woodworking. And the address— Boise, Idaho.

No, she really was being paranoid. The idea that Alan might have hired someone to find her was not something she was willing to dismiss entirely. But that Mack Carlino— a cop on leave, for whatever reason, on his way to Boise— had been sent to find her...it wasn't likely. And it seemed even less likely with each dark, mesmerizing glance of concern Mack gave her during the drive into town.

"This is it." Mack eased the Mustang to a stop alongside the snowbanked curb.

Through the windshield, Teddy eyed the two-story gray clapboard house that had obviously been converted into Doc Wharton's private office. Last night's storm had almost completely covered the painted wooden sign swaying in the icy wind.

Teddy turned her gaze from the house across the street to Mack, as though she might still be able to convince him that she didn't need a doctor. But when Mack shifted in his seat to look at her, he must have read her thoughts. He held up one broad hand to silence her before a single word could leave her lips.

"Teddy, listen. You're going in there, if I have to carry you in." And the look he gave her convinced her that he could, and *would*, carry her in if he had to. After all, hadn't he carried her to her bed last night?

"Fine, Mack. But could we at least check on my Jeep first? The garage is just down the street. In fact, I can see the sign from here." She pointed out the windshield, but Mack didn't follow her gesture. "Look, if you take me there, I can get my car, and then you can be on your way...to Boise."

Mack shook his head. He pulled the parking brake and turned off the engine.

"No dice, darling," he said, dropping his keys in the pocket of his leather bomber jacket. "I'm not going anywhere until I know that you're all right."

Teddy glanced back at the doctor's office and clenched her fists. Mack's chivalrous charm was beginning to wear thin.

"I'm not your responsibility, Mack," Teddy protested, turning to meet his stare once again.

But he didn't have to say anything. There was something in the darkness of his expression, in the stern set of his mouth, that convinced Teddy that Mack blamed himself for what had happened last night. That he *felt* responsible for her. But how could he have known that she'd been trying to lose him in the storm? That she'd suspected him of being connected to Alan?

"Come on," he said at last, and opened his door to a blast of cold air.

Teddy followed suit, stepping out of the Mustang and into a swirl of light crystalline snowflakes that melted instantly on her skin. The heavy soles of her boots squeaked against the hard-packed snow as she walked to the front of the car where Mack waited. When she stepped around the hood of the Mustang, Mack reached over and took her hand.

It was a simple gesture, and yet, Teddy could have sworn that her heart literally stopped when she felt the firmness of his grip through her glove. She had almost fainted earlier, she rationalized. Mack had caught her, and now he was just overly cautious. That's why he took her hand, she concluded. For no other reason...

Why then did she feel much more than a sense of security in his grip? And why did a sudden wave of heat shudder through her body when Mack placed his hand against the small of her back and guided her into the doctor's office?

5

MACK USHERED Teddy into Doc Wharton's small waiting room. The faded vinyl chairs that lined one side of the cheerfully wallpapered room were empty, and if not for the receptionist on the phone behind the front counter, the place would have appeared deserted.

Mack's hand remained firmly against Teddy's back, and even through the heavy lining of her coat, he could feel her body tense. He wondered if it was due to some inherent fear of doctors, or if she was considering the consequences of this visit. It wouldn't have surprised him if Teddy had already foreseen the dangers in seeking medical counsel. He hadn't had an easy time tracking her this far, which was due solely to her deliberate lack of a paper trail. Again, Mack caught himself wondering exactly why Teddy Logan was so desperate not to be found.

"Sorry to keep you waiting," the receptionist apologized as she hung up the phone. She turned her ruddy face toward them and straightened her crisp uniform. "Are you here to see Doc Wharton?"

"Yes, we are," Mack answered, glancing to Teddy at his side. She *did* look better. Perhaps it had been the short walk to the office, but her cheeks held a little more color now, and she didn't seem to need any kind of support as she had back at the cabin.

"All rightee then. I need you to fill out these forms—" The receptionist handed Mack a clipboard and a pen. "Insurance and all that, you know? But the doc should be with you shortly." The phone let out one shrill ring and she turned to pick up the receiver. "Doc Wharton's office..."

With clipboard in hand, Mack started toward the seating area, when he felt Teddy's hand on his arm. He turned to find her rummaging through her purse. "What is it, Teddy?"

"I told you this wasn't a good idea, Mack."

"What?"

"I can't see the doctor."

"Teddy, we've been through this."

"I mean, I don't have my wallet on me. I must have forgotten it at the cabin." She continued to dig through her purse, but Mack knew it was only for effect. So she *had* been one step ahead of him on this. She *knew* she'd have to avoid leaving a paper trail and had purposely left her wallet at the cabin.

"Teddy—"

"I don't have any ID on me, let alone insurance. Look, Mack, it's probably just as well. I'm fine. In fact, I don't even have a headache anymore." She closed her purse and Mack saw her quickly eye the door. "Listen, why don't you just take me to the garage so I can pick up my Jeep?"

"Because I'm not letting you out of here until you see the doctor, Teddy."

But she was already past him and making a beeline for the door, a flurry of Gore-Tex and blond hair.

"Teddy." Mack set the clipboard on the counter and went after her. Whether it was due to the force with which he snatched her arm and spun her around, or the surprise of Doc Wharton's sudden appearance beside them, Teddy's knees suddenly buckled.

In a flash, Mack saw Doc Wharton—his apparent age hindering him not in the least—reach out for Teddy at the same time that Mack's arms encircled her waist. Like this morning, Mack felt her practically crumple against him. Her body slackened for a brief moment of disorientation, then seemed to recover as her hands found his shoulders.

Once she'd righted herself, Teddy did not make any immediate moves to step out of the circle of his arms. Her hands gripped his shoulders and were it not for Doc Wharton's presence, Mack could only guess what might have happened next as he looked down into those enchanting gray eyes and felt the heat of her body against his.

"I guess I'm not so fine, after all," she murmured as though embarrassed by her momentary weakness. Her eyes never left his.

"It's all right, Teddy."

"What seems to be the problem here?"

When Mack was finally able to draw his gaze from Teddy's, he looked to the white-smocked doctor at their side. Doc Wharton slid a pair of bifocals up along the bridge of his nose.

"She's had an accident," Mack started to explain. "Last night. She took her car through a snowbank."

"Ah, yes. You're Sly's friend. He mentioned you'd be in."

Teddy nodded, her hands still on Mack's shoulders.

"I thought it would be best that she come in and get looked at," Mack added. "Just in case."

"Good idea."

"The thing is, we've forgotten her wallet, and without insurance—"

"Oh, let's not worry about paperwork right now, shall we?" Doc Wharton moved in even closer. "I see you've bumped your head. No doubt on the steering wheel, hmm?" he asked, pointing to the dressing on Teddy's forehead.

Teddy nodded again.

"I'm sure it's nothing," she replied.

"You're probably right," Doc said. "But I'm still going to take a look at you, young lady. No one leaves my office without a clean bill of health. I won't have you fainting on my porch. Now, why don't you take off your coat."

TEDDY WATCHED Mack linger in the open doorway of Doc Wharton's office, attempting to look casual with his arms crossed over his chest and his shoulder wedged against the doorjamb. She knew he was anything but relaxed, shifting his weight from one foot to the other, as though he expected her to succumb to another dizzy spell at any moment.

Well, if she had her way, there would be no more fainting. She'd almost made it out the door moments ago, and could have been at the garage by now if it hadn't been for that sudden heady rush that had weakened her knees and sent the room whirling. But the main reason Teddy wanted to avoid another situation like the one in the waiting room was Mack Carlino himself, and because of the sudden, inexplicable feelings that overcame her every time she found herself in his arms—which, by her count, had been two times too often.

The way Mack had looked at her when he'd held her in his arms a short while ago...Teddy could have sworn he wanted to kiss her. But even more shocking was that she had considered it herself. She'd actually found herself excited about the prospect of Mack Carlino kissing her.

She looked past Doc Wharton's shoulder to Mack again. The concern she saw in his expression should have comforted her, but instead it made her uneasy. After all, she'd known the man—consciously speaking—for a mere five hours. How was it that he should display such open and apparently genuine concern for her?

She shifted on the examining table, causing the thin paper cover to crinkle beneath her jeans.

"Well," Doc Wharton mumbled as he lowered his eye scope and took a step back, "I don't think there's any cause for concern at this point. Mind you—" he turned to Mack "—if these dizzy spells persist, I suggest you take her to Craig General for some tests."

Teddy watched Mack nod, wishing she didn't feel like such an invalid.

"As for that cut on your forehead, you might wind up with a slight scar, but it's certainly nothing worthy of my crude stitching skills. Just keep the dressing fresh." Doc Wharton turned his back as he put away his instruments. "So, Sly tells me you're new in town. Are you planning on staying long, Miss—"

Teddy shot a quick look to Mack, wishing that he'd stayed in the waiting room.

"McAllister," she answered quickly, gauging Mack's reaction to her lie, and then surprised at his complete lack of one. "Teddy McAllister. And no, unfortunately I doubt I'll be staying in Birdseye long." Still no reaction from Mack.

"And you're working for Sly?"

"Temporarily, yes."

"Well, perhaps I'll see you at the tavern sometime then, Teddy McAllister. I have been known to sneak in for a brandy on occasion." Doc Wharton gave her an endearing smile that lit up his face.

"Then your next brandy's on me, Doc."

"I'll hold you to it. And until then, you're free to go."

"Thanks, Doc." Teddy eased herself off the examining table and reached for her coat before following him into the waiting room.

"Now, I trust you won't be alone, Teddy?" But the doctor's question was aimed more at Mack than her, Teddy realized as she zipped up her coat. "With head injuries, we always advise that there be someone with you, at least for a day or two, in case—"

"I'll be staying with her, Doc," Mack answered. Teddy's mouth dropped open in an aborted protest. "She'll be in good hands."

"I don't doubt that for one moment." And Teddy caught the doctor's quick wink to Mack. "And don't you go battling any more snowbanks, you hear me, Teddy?"

"Yes, sir," she said with a smile that took as much effort to muster as it did for her to stop from storming out of the office and as far away from Mack Carlino as possible.

Only once they were down the steps and across the street by Mack's car, did Teddy turn on him. Through a cloud of breath vapor that hung fleetingly in the cold air around them, she glared at Mack, trying desperately not to notice how the late-morning sun warmed his handsome features and practically gleamed off his instantly faltering smile.

"You didn't have to do that, Mack," she blurted out, jamming her hands into her gloves.

"Do what?"

"Tell him that I'm in good hands. That you're going to stay with me."

"But I am."

"No. You're not."

"You heard what he said, Teddy. Someone has to—"

"I heard what he said. But you don't need to stay. I can spend the night in town. And tomorrow night too, if I have to. I'll stay with Sly, or my friend Maryanne."

There was a perceptible shift behind his gaze as his eyes narrowed and his mouth tightened, and in that moment Teddy could have sworn that Mack saw right through her. He knew she was lying. Yes, there was no doubt in her mind—Mack Carlino must have been one hell of a good cop.

"I think it would be better if I stayed," he said simply. "Like Doc Wharton suggested. Now, would you like me to take you to the garage?"

He didn't wait for her answer, but instead unlocked the driver's-side door and got in. She saw him reach across to unlock her door before he started the Mustang's engine.

"Fine," she muttered under her breath, walking around to the passenger's side. And at that moment, Teddy realized that a part of her despised Mack Carlino—despised him for being able to read her like a book, and despised him for the inexplicable chaos of emotions that overcame her whenever he so much as looked at her with those deep, dark eyes of his.

It was going to be a long couple of days.

"I TELL YA, Teddy, she don't look too good. What you done to this ol' girl, well, she's not happy." Graham Tock rapped a large wrench along the underside of Teddy's hoisted Jeep and shook his head with all the gravity one would expect from a funeral director.

Teddy managed a smile. "Get to the point, Graham, or the next beer I serve you ends up in your lap. What's this going to cost? And how long am I going to have to wait?"

A rough grin turned up one corner of his long unshaven face. "Well, you're looking at an alignment, a new stabilizing rod in the front, a couple new tires and rims on the right there and a new headlamp. And that's just to see her on the road again."

"How long, Graham?"

"Parts should be here soon. Prob'ly have her ready for ya tomorrow afternoon."

Teddy shook her head as she walked around to the front

of the hoist and scrutinized the Jeep's battered grill and dented bumper. When she and Mack had walked into Graham Tock's garage, she'd been expecting to find the Jeep in far worse condition, so initially she'd been relieved. But when she gazed up at the front of the vehicle, where it had sustained most of the damage, the full shock of the accident hit home.

She certainly didn't need Graham's opinions now to ease her mind.

"Let me say one thing, Teddy. You were lucky," he said. "Damned lucky. You coulda taken her right down the mountainside, ya know? Or smashed the windshield ta bits or somethin'. And then to have Mack here find you... Hell, if he hadn't'a come along, you coulda froze up there! You had that front end buried so deep no one woulda seen ya till mornin' at least. It's a downright miracle, I tell ya."

Mack must have noticed the slight shiver that trembled through her as she recognized the truth behind Graham's analysis. She felt Mack move up behind her and place one hand on her shoulder. In light of the shock she felt now, it was easy to accept his comfort.

"Are you all right?" Mack whispered close to her ear.

She nodded, her gaze fixed on the Jeep. Yes, Graham was right. She *had* been lucky. And Mack had been her miracle. Her guardian angel.

"'Course," Graham continued, running one grease-stained hand along the front bumper, "if you'll be wantin' me ta take them dents outta this chrome bumper here—"

"Forget the dents, Graham. How much is all this going to cost me?

"Nuttin'."

"Nothing? And how do you come up with that figure?"

"From Sly."

"I'm not following you, Graham. What's going on?"

"Sly took care of it."

"What? What do you mean he took care of it? How much is it?"

"Can't say."

"Why not?"

"Sly told me it was taken care of, and that I wasn't sup-posed to let you argue 'bout it."

"No, wait, I don't—"

"Look, doll, Sly says he feels responsible, see? Says he should'na never have let you drive up there last night, is what he says. So he took care of it."

Mack's hand tightened on her shoulder as though he un-derstood her discomfort with Sly's generosity. Through the open garage doors and across the street, Teddy could see Sly's bar. The red neon Open sign flickered in the front win-dow.

"Well, thanks, Graham," she said at last. "I guess this is something I have to take up with Sly myself. Tomorrow af-ternoon, right?"

"I'll have her ready for ya."

SLY'S TAVERN accommodated a fair-size lunch crowd. No doubt because it was the only place in Birdseye that served up a midday beer. From his position on the end stool, Mack had a good vantage point from which to view the bar and tables, but his attention was riveted on Teddy.

He cradled his mug of black coffee between his hands and watched her argue with Sly at the far end of the bar. He couldn't make out their words, but he didn't need to. Mo-ments ago Sly had attempted to hand Teddy a few rumpled bills, obviously last week's pay, and Mack had watched her shake her head adamantly, refusing the money. It was when Sly had started to shake his head, as well, and press the bills back into her hands, that Teddy's argument became more animated. Her slender hands worked the air between them, slashing and gesturing with each word, and Mack suspected it was about the Jeep.

He also suspected that it wasn't easy for Teddy to accept the generosity of others. Born into Logan wealth, she'd probably never had to turn to anyone before, certainly not for any kind of financial assistance.

Mack took a sip of coffee and smiled. He rather enjoyed seeing Teddy's sparked ire. He admired her resolve and the spirit in her that refused to accept charity. But without Sly's handout, Teddy no doubt realized, she would have to resort to using credit cards, and that would lead Alan Somerton right to her.

Mack only wished he could tell Teddy that she'd already been found, that one phone call separated her from her fiancé. Then again, the more he came to know Teddy, the more determined he was not to place that phone call until he'd learned her side of the story.

"Saw ya in here last night." The raspy voice cut through Mack's thoughts. He pulled his gaze from Teddy to the bear of a man who commandeered the stool next to his. "Mind if I join ya?"

"Not at all," Mack said.

"Bill Hensley," the man said. "I run the hardware store down the street."

"Mack Carlino."

"So you just passing through?"

"That's right."

"You a friend of Teddy's?" Hensley nodded to where she still argued with Sly. "I noticed you come in with her today."

"Actually, we've only just met."

"Oh, that's too bad."

"How's that?"

"Well, it's just, see, me and some of the boys here, we've got a wager going."

"On what? Teddy?"

"Sorta. See, we were hoping you could offer us a little insight."

"Let me get this straight," Mack asked, amused at the notion that these grown men could be so preoccupied with Teddy Logan that they'd actually taken to wagering on her. "You have a bet going on Teddy."

"Yeah. Kinda like what we think she's doin' here, where she's from. That sort of thing. She's so damned secretive, that one. It's drivin' us nuts, ya know?"

Mack nodded. At the other end of the bar, Teddy swept a hand through her hair, a gleaming motion of gold and blond. And when she turned her head to follow Sly's nod, Mack could have sworn he felt the cool touch of those eyes clear across the room.

"Yes," he admitted at last, "I know what you mean, Bill."

TEDDY DIDN'T LIKE losing arguments, but there had been no winning with Sly. Only when he'd agreed to let her repay him eventually for the repairs to the Jeep, did she accept half of the pay he tried to give her. She needed the cash. She hated that fact, but until she was ready to go back to Denver and face the music, she couldn't risk using her credit cards.

When she'd finally shoved the few bills into the front pocket of her jeans, Teddy had glanced up to find Mack staring at her. She wondered if he'd heard her argument with Sly, or if he would question her about it later.

Then again, Mack hadn't asked many questions at all—no more than a fleeting inquiry as to her reasons for being in Birdseye. In fact, he hadn't even questioned her use of a false name back at Doc Wharton's office. For a cop, he certainly wasn't big on interrogation. Teddy supposed she should consider herself fortunate—the last thing she needed was a cross-examination.

"So, Sly tells me this Mack guy is going to be staying with you?" Maryanne had come out of nowhere, sidled up beside Teddy and nodded toward Mack.

"Word travels fast," Teddy answered her.

"'Round here 'fast' is relative. Remember, this is Birdseye—word doesn't have too far to go. But, Teddy, correct me if I'm wrong, isn't Sly's cabin a one-bedroom?"

"Yes. And I can assure you that it comes with a very comfortable couch. Besides, it's doctor's orders. And, if I have my way, he'll be gone by morning."

"So are you going to tell me what happened last night? I mean, the part you didn't tell Sly?" Maryanne took several beers from the bar fridge and set them on her tray.

"There's nothing to tell, Maryanne. Honestly. In fact, I don't remember anything about it. The last thing I remember was the Jeep flying off the road. And then I woke up this morning."

"In bed?"

"No, on the kitchen table, Maryanne. Of course, in bed!"

Maryanne's voice was reduced to a hushed whisper as she cleverly directed her gaze past Teddy's shoulder to gain a clear view of Mack.

"So did he...did he undress you?"

Teddy felt the familiar flush as she once again imagined Mack taking care of her last night. "Yes, I suppose he did. I'm rather certain that it wasn't Bogie."

The mischievous smile that was an almost permanent fixture on Maryanne's young face slipped by a degree. But it was the seriousness of her expression, as Maryanne continued to gawk at Mack at the end of the bar, that concerned Teddy.

"What is it, Maryanne?"

"Are you sure, Teddy?"

"'Sure'? What do you mean? Sure that Bogie didn't undress me last night? I think I'm pretty sure—"

"No, I mean about this guy. Mack Carlino. Is he...okay?"

Teddy followed her friend's gaze to where Mack had
taken up a conversation with Bill Hensley. Seeing Mack in
this light, smiling, conversing with the hardware-store
owner, so apparently at ease, Teddy wondered how someone she barely knew could appear so suddenly familiar,
seem so instantly honorable.

Yet, Maryanne's question was a valid one. And for the
first time, Teddy realized that she hadn't questioned Mack
Carlino's integrity. After all, his was a face she hadn't even
seen before last night. And yet, she hadn't even doubted his
intentions. She'd automatically believed them sincere.

Was it instinct? Or foolishness?

"Teddy? What do you know about him?"

She looked back at Maryanne and shook her head. "I
know he's from Denver and that he is...was a cop."

"Is that enough for you to trust him?"

"He saved my life last night, Maryanne." When she
glanced over her shoulder this time, Mack met her gaze and
Teddy returned his quick smile.

"As long as you're sure, Teddy," Maryanne said, tucking
her tray against her hip and heading through the bar gate to
do her rounds.

But "sure" was the last thing Teddy was.

Yes, seeing his brother's business card on the dash of
Mack's Mustang had eased her suspicions. But more than
Mack Carlino's identity, more than his reason for being in
Birdseye or his motive in following her last night, the thing
Teddy was the *least* sure about was the feelings that con-
sumed her when he merely looked her way. Or the thoughts
that raced through her mind when she'd found herself in his

arms at Doc Wharton's office. And given the fantasies she'd already entertained about him, she *certainly* wasn't sure about spending the night in a one-bedroom cabin with the man.

6

MACK GAVE THE POT of tomato sauce another stir and savored the sweet aroma that permeated the cabin. After leaving Sly's, he and Teddy had gone to the grocer's, where Mack had insisted on buying the ingredients for a true Italian dinner, he promised Teddy, the likes of which she'd never experienced. Now, gazing down at the bubbling and congealing red mass, he prayed it would taste even half as good as it smelled. Luckily, he'd picked up more than a few pointers growing up in an Irish-Italian household. Still, it had been a while since he'd cooked for anyone, let alone someone with the kind of cultured tastes that Teddy Logan undoubtedly possessed.

He replaced the lid and looked once again out the window over the sink. Past the cabin's porch and the clearing beyond the driveway, Mack's gaze followed a thin, meandering path through the waist-high snow. At the end of it was Teddy.

Bundled in her coat and scarf, leggings and a pair of wool socks bunched up over the tops of her boots, she paced the partially cleared dock overlooking the small frozen lake. At the other end of the dock, Bogie sat patiently, watching her, as well, a stick dangling from his massive jaws. She'd been out there for so long that Mack had begun to wonder if he should go out and get her.

But, no. She needed her space. He was certain of that.

It had been a close call, he thought as he cast a glance

across the cabin to the wooden desk in the corner. They had been back at the cabin for less than two hours when he'd almost been caught. After putting away the groceries and showing Mack around the kitchen, Teddy had taken him up on his advice to lie down. She'd looked tired and drawn. And once the bedroom door had closed, Mack had concentrated on starting dinner.

With the sauce simmering on the back burner, however, he had taken to nosing around the cabin, hoping to discover an explanation for Teddy's flight from Denver and the reason Alan Somerton was so determined to find her. Mack had eyed the laptop computer on the corner desk, but instead turned his attention to the papers and notes around it. His limited experience had taught him to give computers a wide berth.

As he leafed through pages of elegant handwriting, it was obvious that even though Teddy had extricated herself from her life in Denver, Logan Publishing was not something she could completely abandon. There were notes to herself, memos and reminders of issues she obviously planned to address and ideas she intended to initiate upon her return.

But nothing about Alan Somerton.

Scrawled on the corner of some diner take-out menu, Mack had found a name and address: Holly, 15 Paseo Drive, Fort Collins. He'd made a mental note of it, and had started to dig further when he'd heard the bedroom door unlatch behind him.

He was certain that he'd stepped away from the desk quickly enough, but when he turned to greet her, a hint of suspicion flickered faintly in her eyes. He hadn't seen that look since this morning. His brother's business card had seemed to ease Teddy's suspicions, and Mack had prided himself on planting the card strategically on the Mustang's dash this morning when he'd gone out to clean off the car.

From the corner of his eye, he'd seen her check out the card, and afterward, her apprehension had almost visibly calmed. Until she'd seen him standing near her desk.

"Dinner smells good," she'd said as she reached for her coat, but her voice sounded flat. When she'd told him she was going out for a walk, Mack knew she had meant alone.

And so far he'd respected that. But an hour? Surely she was cold out there. He looked again through the window. The sky had dimmed. The setting sun was cloaked by snow-laden clouds. A burst of wind caught Teddy's hair and whipped it back from her face as she stared out across the lake's frozen surface. Bogie joined her now, his tail wagging. Mack watched as she reached down, took the stick from the dog's mouth and tossed it. The big dog bounded through the deep snow in pursuit, and Teddy turned her back to the cabin once more, her arms crossed over her chest.

What was going through her mind as she looked out over that expanse of snow and ice? Was she thinking of Denver? Was she thinking of Alan Somerton?

He'd spent less than a day with her, and yet Mack felt as though he knew Teddy. He'd witnessed her strength of character, and was convinced that she wasn't the type of person to run from a fight. There had to be more behind her leaving Denver than her fiancé had let on.

Somerton had called it a "tiff." A lovers' quarrel. And then he'd gone on to tell Mack how worried he was about Teddy being on her own, how vulnerable she was. It hardly sounded like the Teddy who Mack had come to know.

But he'd been suspicious of Somerton from the moment the man had walked into Mack's office. Maybe it was Somerton's too-trim veneer, his perfectly pressed suit and his fastidiously manicured hands, or perhaps it had been the quick defensiveness that appeared in Alan's manner when Mack had suggested Somerton simply wait for his fiancée to return on her own. And that defensiveness had doubled when Mack asked if Teddy had broken off their engagement.

Somerton's voice had risen steadily as he'd told Mack that it was only a disagreement and that she would never break their engagement. Yet Mack had already seen Teddy's diamond ring—not on her finger, but on the nightstand by her bed.

Even now, miles away from Denver and Somerton, the man left a bad taste in Mack's mouth. If his agency didn't need a good shot of revenue right now, Mack would never have accepted the assignment. But when Somerton started pulling bills out of his wallet—crisp one-hundreds—Mack knew he'd be a fool to decline.

He cast one more glance at Teddy out on the dock—she hadn't moved. Yes, he decided, she was probably thinking of Somerton. And Mack found himself wondering again how an exceptional woman like Teddy Logan had ended up with a man like Alan Somerton.

Mack crossed the kitchen to the phone. As he jabbed at the number pad, he realized that he should have called Blake Tennyson a week ago. His ex-partner could run a check on Alan Somerton and see if anything turned up on the guy. As unlikely as that was, it was worth a phone call at least. Mack only wished that he'd thought of it before he'd ever left Denver to find Teddy.

STARING OUT over the wide expanse of frozen lake, Teddy watched the first heavy flakes drift quietly down from the steel-gray sky. That was the one thing that struck her most profoundly about this place, she thought—the silence...the still, almost ear-ringing, silence. And the peace. It was a peace she'd never felt in Denver; a peace she'd not found with Alan. At least, not lately.

Almost instinctively her left hand curled up inside her glove and she felt the nakedness of her ring finger. She thought about the engagement ring in the cabin, on her nightstand. In spite of everything, Teddy could still remember her joy when he'd given her the ring and asked her to be his wife. He'd loved her—back then there hadn't been any question in her mind. He'd slipped that ring onto her finger and she'd been able to visualize their whole life unfolding together.

But now, with Alan's ever-growing obsession with Logan Publishing and his work…that love, and that vision, was not as apparent as it had once been. Yes, their engagement had become rocky even before their confrontation in Alan's office a month ago. He'd started working through weekends and holidays, to the point where Logan Publishing was his world, and his relationship with Teddy merely another component of "the big Logan picture." And the greater his obsession grew, the greater the distance between them, and the less Teddy was able to imagine wearing Alan's engagement ring again.

She almost couldn't recall the way it had once felt on her finger. And the longer she stayed away from Alan, the louder the whispers of doubt echoed in her mind.

The strange thing was, up until now, Teddy hadn't allowed herself the time to doubt her relationship with Alan. Things simply went on. The company took most of her energy, as it did Alan's, and questioning the engagement would only have forced Teddy to question her entire life and all the choices she'd made—right or wrong. It had been easier just to follow the flow.

But a month away from all that…it certainly provided a new perspective. What worried her, though, was that all of a sudden this new perspective included Mack Carlino. Life had seemed so much clearer even yesterday, before she'd met Mack.

Teddy turned to look back at the cabin. Large flakes brushed against her face before melting. She drew in a deep breath of the crisp, clean air.

Yes, before Mack Carlino had blown out of the storm and into her life, with his magnetic smile and handsome ruggedness, with his inarguable concern and infuriating ability to send her emotions reeling, life had been complicated. But not nearly as complicated as it was now.

MACK WAS CERTAIN his knuckles were white around the receiver as he listened to Blake's ranting. At first he'd considered himself lucky to find his ex-partner at the downtown headquarters, but now Mack was having reservations on that count.

After Mack had filled in his ex-partner on his dealings with Alan Somerton, Blake had agreed that running a check on the guy wasn't such a bad idea. More than anyone, Blake Tennyson trusted Mack's instincts. But then Blake had demanded to know where Mack was calling from, and when Mack at last fessed up, the verbal finger-waggling had commenced. He should have hung up then; instead, he'd let his ex-partner have his say. And now, ten minutes later, Blake Tennyson was still having it.

"I just hate to see you do it again, Mack."

"Do what?"

"Get personally involved in a case. Hasn't experience taught you anything?"

"Blake—"

"Don't screw around, Mack."

"I'm not. Listen to me, there are two sides to this story, and until I get Teddy's side, I'm not about to just turn her in to this guy. He's off, Blake, I tell you. He's fishy. I don't know what he's up to, but it's definitely something."

"So, are you telling me her life could be in danger?"

"No, but—"

"Then get the hell out of there. Wash your hands of it, pal. Wash your hands of *her*."

"I can't do that."

There was a long silence, and Mack envisioned his best friend sitting at his desk, using the heel of his hand to rub his right eye—his one good eye. Over the left, Blake had worn a patch for the past two years. Ever since the shooting. No doubt, Blake was thinking of that right now, as was Mack.

"Look," Blake said at last, letting out a long breath. "I'll check out this Somerton guy for you, okay? If I come up with anything, I'll leave it with your secretary."

"Thanks, Blake. I owe you one."

"Just promise me you won't do anything stupid."

As Mack hung up the phone, he knew exactly what Blake was talking about. The trouble was, Mack was beginning to fear that keeping a promise like that was completely beyond his control. After all, his getting involved with Teddy was becoming far more than mere fantasy.

"No, seriously, Mack. I'm not just saying it to be nice," Teddy shouted from the living room to the kitchen where Mack was finishing the last of the washing up. "That had to be *the* best spaghetti dinner ever."

Next to where she sat on the rug in front of the couch, Bogie sprawled out across the floorboards. She lowered a hand to his massive head and watched the big dog's eyes close slowly as she ran her fingers through the thick fur. Like Teddy, he basked in the heat of a massive blaze that hissed and crackled in the flagstone hearth before them. In fact, Teddy thought, the fire that Mack had started an hour ago had more than adequately warmed the cabin, and for the first time since her arrival in Birdseye she found herself in a T-shirt.

When Mack came into the living room, Teddy noticed that he too had shed his heavy wool sweater and was down to a cotton shirt with the cuffs rolled up. In one hand he carried the bottle of Chianti they'd started at dinner, and he refilled both their glasses before turning his attention to the fire.

"I think we can let this die down a bit," he suggested, taking up a fire iron from the huge flagstone hearth.

Teddy nodded. "This is definitely a case where the mason overestimated the size of the cabin, wouldn't you say?"

Mack's laughter rolled easily from his throat. Teddy liked its comforting lilt. As Mack squatted before the roaring blaze, she watched his strong arms work the iron between the crackling logs to separate them. And as the flames settled to a warm, flickering glow, she once again considered the cozy domesticity of the evening—first the dinner, then the dishes, and finally settling with a bottle of wine in front of the fire. A lifetime away from the hollow vastness of the Logan estate, with its hired help and its prepared meals. Staring at Mack again, Teddy realized that she could get used to this kind of life-style.

When Mack turned at last, Teddy gave him a brief smile and looked quickly to the hearth again, embarrassed by her daydreams. He lowered himself to the floor next to her and handed her a wineglass. She swirled the dark crimson liquid, watching the reflection of the flames circle slowly, and contemplated the wisdom of drinking any more. Given her current light-headedness, Teddy doubted it would take much before all of her inhibitions were completely stripped away.

"So, Mack." Talk, she decided. Yes, talk would eradicate the lustful thoughts that tortured her in Mack's overwhelming closeness. "How many years were you a cop?"

She glanced over at him, less than two feet away, and watched him smile over the rim of his glass. It was a smile of amusement, and she knew he'd recognized her tactic.

"Twelve years," he answered.

"So why the leave? Twelve years hardly seems like a career one tosses aside lightly."

"No, it's not." He shook his head, and turned his gaze to the fire as though letting the dancing flames take him back to a time he would sooner forget. As she studied his chiseled profile, Teddy thought she saw the glimmer of distant pain. A muscle along his strong jaw clenched a couple of times, and she had the sudden urge to reach out and touch it, to nestle her palm against his cheek and calm the old hurt that darkened his expression.

When he finally spoke, his voice held a note of pain. "Two years ago I got my partner shot. We'd been working together in undercover narcotics for a few years. At the time, we were collaborating with the FBI, closing in on the head of a major cartel that reached from Denver all the way to the West Coast. Blake and I spent a year squeezing our way up the ranks, informant by informant. And then I screwed up."

Teddy kept silent. She didn't have to prompt him now. For some reason, Mack seemed comfortable and willing to divulge a part of his past she doubted he'd shared with many.

"There was this woman. We'd been relying heavily on her alliance with several of the higher-ups in the cartel, but we'd underestimated the depth that her connections ran. Or rather, *I* underestimated *her*. I let emotions get in the way. Everything I'd learned about the job, I threw out the window. I honestly believed that I could stay on top of things.

Before I knew it, I'd gotten in so deep I'd lost complete touch with the job. I ignored all of my partner's warnings, figuring I could handle things, that I could maintain my focus, my perspective. And by the time I realized that I couldn't...it was too late."

He combed his fingers through his sleek jet-black hair and let out a long breath.

"We did manage to bring the cartel down, but it wasn't a clean job. I'd messed up, and my personal involvement with this informant almost got my partner killed. He took two bullets. One was a flesh wound to the hip, but the other...the other took his left eye. It could have just as easily taken Blake's life."

Mack tipped back his glass and drained the last of his wine. "No one but Blake really knew how I'd screwed up. I think that was the hardest thing of all—the fact that he'd kept quiet about the whole thing. The situation might have been easier for me to deal with if I'd been reprimanded or forced to resign. But nothing happened. So I took an indefinite leave."

He reached for the bottle and refilled his glass before turning his dark gaze onto Teddy once again.

"Yeah," he said, "Regrets...I guess I've got a few of those."

"And what about life off the force?"

He shrugged. "A bit of this, a bit of that. At first I taught part-time. Courses at the academy. It paid the bills. Then I started working at an indoor shooting range. Gave lessons, that sort of thing."

"And now carpentry?"

A smile lit up his face as he shifted to face her. "And exactly what is wrong with carpentry?"

"Nothing. It's just...from undercover narcotics to carpentry? Hard to believe."

"You don't believe me? Well, I'll have you know that I'm one helluva carpenter. Learned everything from my father—handiest man with a chisel in all of Little Italy, he was."

"In New York City?"

Mack nodded and the smile that touched his lips held what Teddy could only imagine were fond memories. "Yeah, well, mine wasn't exactly a glamorous life. Just your average blue-collar upbringing on the other side of Canal Street, you know."

"So why Denver?"

"I don't know. Guess I just wanted a change of scenery. I left my father's carpentry business and moved to Colorado when I was nineteen. Been here ever since. But what about you?"

"What about me?"

"What's your story?"

"*My* story?" Teddy looked away from him, unable to meet that penetrating gaze.

"Yeah. Frankly, I'm still trying to figure *that* one out. I mean, Birdseye? Come on, Teddy, there's more to you than this." He waved his hand to indicate the rest of the cabin that lay in darkness behind their intimate fireside nest.

It was Teddy's turn to have her glass refilled. Letting the wine roll over her tongue and warm her throat, she felt the edges of her well-guarded dam crumbling. But it wasn't only the wine, she realized. It was Mack's candidness about his own past that prompted her now; his honesty and his obvious trust in her inspired her to do the same.

"Well, I'm not usually a bartender."

"Really? I'm shocked." He flashed her a smirk. "So where *did* you learn to sling beers?"

"Actually, during my Yale years."

"Yale? Wow."

"What? You thought I was just another dumb blonde from Denver?"

"Actually, no. Not at all. I didn't know you were from Denver."

Bogie raised his head off the floorboards long enough to cast a bleary gaze at the two of them as they laughed.

"So Yale, hmm?" Mack asked finally. "No kidding?"

"No kidding. But don't rush to congratulate me. I never finished."

"Why not?"

"My father." If she'd actually *wanted* to put a damper on the mood, Teddy realized, she couldn't have done it any faster than she just had. She took a deep breath, turned her gaze to her wineglass and told Mack about Logan Publishing. He admitted his recognition of the name and seemed surprised to find out that Teddy was part of the Logan empire. She told Mack of her mother's death when Teddy was thirteen, and the years she'd spent struggling with that loss. And then she'd talked about her father, how her mother's death had taken its toll on him, as well, and how he'd thrown himself into Logan Publishing as though there was nothing else in his world. And when she told Mack about her father's heart attack three years ago and how she'd left Yale to return to the company, she recognized the faintest trace of bitterness in her voice.

"Yes, I suppose you could say that I hate Logan Publishing for that. For taking me away from what I loved, from the future I had at Yale. I do resent it, but I also have a future at Logan." Teddy wished that her words hadn't sounded as if she'd just given herself a pep talk.

"So, is that what you're running away from—the company?"

Teddy turned to face him, her elbow wedged against the seat of the couch, and probed his dark eyes, half expecting to see the wheels spinning inside Mack Carlino's head. How could anyone be so damnably intuitive?

"And why would you assume I'm running away?"

"McAllister," he said simply. "You gave the doctor a false name. I'm assuming that's the one you're using up here, while you tend bar? Teddy McAllister?"

"All right. You win. But I'm not running away. Let's just say I needed a break. And...I don't exactly want to be found."

"Found by whom?"

Dare she answer that one? Hadn't she already said enough?

But then Mack answered it for her. "Is it your fiancé?"

"How...?" Suspicion trickled down her spine again—from the back of her mind she heard the same niggling voice that had spoken to her last night when she'd seen Mack's headlights. "How...how is it that you know so much about me, Mack Carlino?"

"I don't actually," he said with a casual shrug. "I saw the diamond on your bedside table. And I noticed the faint tan line on your ring finger where you've obviously worn it. So, I'm assuming you've been engaged for several months at least?"

It was a valid enough explanation. It made sense that someone with Mack's training would put those few pieces together, Teddy thought as she tried to push back her distrust again. "Once a cop, always a cop, is that it?"

Mack shrugged again.

"Yes, Alan and I...have been engaged for almost ten months. We actually met two years ago when he joined Logan Publishing. He started out in the accounting department and now he's practically my father's right-hand man. His golden boy, in fact. Of course, along with that position, it seems, comes the unwritten prerequisite that he be as un-remittingly engrossed in the business as my father is."

Mack offered a nod, nothing more.

"I don't know, maybe it's just a phase Alan's going through. It's almost like he's trying to prove something with his work. I keep thinking he'll snap out of it and be his old self again."

"So is that why you left? To give him time to 'snap out of it'? You figure you'll go home and find the old Alan waiting for you?"

Teddy let out a short laugh. "I think there's a better chance of that lake outside thawing tonight than there is of Alan ever changing." She looked at the fire again. "No, Mack, I left because I needed to. I needed time for myself."

"So why the cloak-and-dagger routine?"

"Alan."

Mack remained silent.

"You don't know him," she continued. "If he wants to find me, he'll go to any lengths to do it. Once Alan gets something in his head...he gets obsessed. In fact, last night, when I saw your headlights in my rearview mirror...I half thought that you might be Alan. Or someone he'd hired to find me."

Teddy gauged Mack's reaction. She didn't want to believe that his passing through Birdseye was anything but inno-cent, that his "intuitiveness" was nothing more than the workings of a cop's mind. Yet she couldn't simply dismiss the paranoia, and a small part of her almost expected to see something in Mack's face that would confirm her needling suspicion. But the dark expression he turned on her held no answers.

"I know," she said at last, letting out a long breath, "para-noid, right?"

Mack shook his head and the silence deepened. She was

grateful when he finally spoke. "Well, Teddy Logan, a.k.a. McAllister, you lead a very complicated life."

"Not at all like a carpenter's, huh?"

He held her stare, and she watched a breathtaking smile curve his lips and send a soft warmth rippling up to his eyes. "No. Definitely not like a carpenter's."

And then, as though it had been building without her even being aware, the air between them seemed thick with an almost electric pulsing—like an ethereal heartbeat, belonging to neither of them, but instead to the very air around them. It vibrated in the fragile space that separated them, drawing them together like some irreversible force.

Mack was so close to her. Inches away. Teddy swore she felt his breath whisper down across her hand where she held her wineglass. And his eyes, those great brown depths that seemed bottomless...she could get lost in them.

No. It had to be the wine, Teddy thought, clinging to her last shred of reason. Or maybe even the blow to the head she'd suffered. She couldn't be having these kinds of impassioned cravings for a man she'd only just met. She'd not even really looked at another man since meeting Alan.

She drew away from Mack, feeling the pulse calm but not cease. And she wondered if he had felt the vibration, as well.

"So, Yale, huh?" There was a waver of frustration in Mack's voice.

Teddy nodded, turning her gaze back to the fire.

"Do you think you'll ever go back?"

"I'd like to." She struggled to find her voice. "I'd like to finish my law degree. Not that I wouldn't return to Logan Publishing once I was done. It's only that finishing my degree is something I've really wanted to do."

"Then you should."

One of the logs in the hearth settled and a cloud of sparks flared briefly before disappearing up the chimney.

"I guess at one point," Teddy went on, "I had hoped that I could rely on Alan more. I figured that once we married, he could assume more responsibility within the company so that I could go back and finish."

"And you don't see that happening now?"

Even to her closest friend, Holly, Teddy hadn't admitted her fear, she realized as she watched hesitant flames lick at one of the logs. It *had* to be the wine.

"Let's just say that I'm having more and more difficulty imagining that scenario ever happening."

"You don't trust Alan?"

"With the company?" She shrugged. "Sure I do. Logan Publishing means the world to him. I just have trouble seeing..." She couldn't say it. It didn't matter how many times Teddy had felt it over the past few months, she'd never spoken the one truth that she could barely admit to *herself*.

When Mack's hand settled on her shoulder, Teddy was amazed at how natural the gesture seemed. How could his touch, at one moment so electric and so overwhelmingly provocative, be so familiar? So affectionate? Like the comforting touch of a longtime lover.

"What is it you have trouble seeing, Teddy?" he asked, as if he could wave a magic wand and grant her that one wish, the answer to all of her doubts.

"The whole neat and tidy picture," she confessed at last. "But especially...me marrying Alan."

She expected to find herself swimming in those dark eyes of Mack's once again when she looked up from her glass. Instead, he studied the fire, the low orange flicker warming his stern expression.

"I haven't told anyone else that." Her admission came out

in a whisper. "I...I think I've felt it for a long time, but I've never spoken it."

Still, Mack's gaze remained fixed on the hearth, and Teddy wondered if he too felt the pulse reawakening, stirring the air around them. She wondered if Mack knew, as she did, that the second he looked at her, they would almost certainly be lost.

"Maybe it's easier to tell a stranger." His voice embraced the silence of the cabin. "Maybe it's easier to tell someone who's only passing through your life."

"Are you, Mack? Are you only passing through?"

In that instant, as Mack turned the full power of his magnetic gaze onto her, Teddy knew he was going to kiss her. The air hummed, and the pulse between them quickened. And suddenly there was nothing—no past, no future, only the here and now. Only Mack and her. Even the fire crackling in the hearth seemed nothing compared to the blaze that drew them together.

And as Mack leaned closer, his hand sliding from her shoulder to the nape of her neck, Teddy realized that she wanted him to kiss her; that she'd wanted his kiss all day, even though she hadn't been able to admit it to herself until this moment.

In the same way that her Jeep had careened off the road last night—that same blinding, headlong rush—Teddy felt herself propelled toward Mack now. Powerless and completely out of control.

7

SHE WOULD HAVE THOUGHT herself prepared for Mack's kiss. She'd seen it coming. She'd yearned for it. Imagined it. And yet, even as he wove his fingers through her hair and caught her chin with his other hand, tilting her face toward his, even as she felt his breath whisper across her cheek...Teddy hadn't been ready for the heart-stopping moment when Mack's lips brushed hers.

It was barely a touch. In fact, Teddy wondered if he'd actually kissed her or if she'd merely imagined it. So light. So gentle, as though he was testing her, giving her time to change her mind. But the hot shiver that coursed through her when she felt him move closer convinced Teddy that there was no way she *could* have changed her mind—she wanted this as much as Mack seemed to.

She reached for him and her hand met the solidness of his wide chest beneath his cotton shirt. Under her palm she felt the quickening of his heart, as rapid as her own, and as her hand traveled toward his shoulder, she felt the hard ripple of muscle. Straining—as though bridling an unfathomable hunger.

His lips touched hers again, an intimate embrace that contradicted the powerful yearning she felt locked in each quivering muscle her hand caressed. And when her fingers fanned back through his sleek hair, Teddy threw herself into the urgency of their kiss.

She wondered if she'd forgotten how to breathe, as his

mouth claimed hers with an almost crushing force. There was no more hesitation. His tongue cleverly traced the line of her willing lips, parting them easily, and then moving inside her mouth. She kissed him, as well—tasting, probing, drinking in his desire. She was alive with anticipation. More alive than she had ever felt.

And his hands...his wide, strong hands were magic. As he moved closer, the power of his body was almost overwhelming as Teddy felt his touch through the thin cotton of her T-shirt. His fingers traced across her shoulders and back, following her spine to where her jeans hugged her hips. And when he slid his hand beneath the thin fabric, Teddy heard her own small gasp slip from her throat. He moved his hand steadily upward, exploring every curve and angle as though he'd waited a long time to do so and intended to savor the experience. It moved past her stomach and her rib cage, until finally she felt him finger her bra and cup one lace-clad breast.

He shifted over her now, kneeling between her legs, as he deftly pulled the rest of her T-shirt from her jeans. In one fluid movement, the T-shirt was gone, and in its place were Mack's arms, cradling her, lowering her to the soft rug beneath them. Vaguely, Teddy was aware of the fire in the hearth and its warmth against her exposed skin, but even that felt cool in comparison to the heat of Mack's lips.

Such skillful lips, she thought, as his kisses burned along the sensitive skin of her throat, her temple, and then behind her ear, each one sending a desperate shudder through her. It was as if Mack had kissed her a million times, as if he'd been given some map that detailed every point along Teddy's body that was sure to melt. Yet it was all so new, so exhilarating, like nothing she'd ever experienced...or could have ever imagined. And when his kisses fanned downward, when Mack pulled back the thin lace of her bra and his lips seared against one nipple, Teddy heard a low guttural moan that could have been her own, or Mack's, or both.

She wanted to feel him. Needed to feel the heat of his body blaze along her skin, as hot as those lips, as powerful as those hands. As though sensing her desire, Mack eased back, drawing away just far enough that Teddy could undo the buttons of his shirt and tug it free from the waistband of his jeans. It was then, as she brushed aside the cool cotton and watched the firelight dance across each defined muscle that seemed to have been chiseled into Mack's tanned torso and chest, that Teddy heard one word flit through her mind.

Forbidden.

She pushed the thought away, forcing it back into the darkness, and reached out for Mack. Her breath locked in her throat and her thighs felt like molten liquid as her fingertips brushed across taut, smooth skin. She caressed the tension of each muscle, trailing her hands steadily upward, over the soft mat of black hair across his chest, past his wide shoulders and finally around to the back of his neck. Teddy pulled him to her, drawing his mouth to hers again, knowing that she was treading on dangerous territory, but powerless to turn back.

As she glided her hands down his back and at last felt the breathtaking fire of his naked skin against hers, Teddy once again heard that little voice in her head. This time, it reminded her where and *who* she was, and whose mouth she so fervently kissed. It screamed at her as she fingered the top button of Mack's jeans and knew that she wanted more, that she wanted everything Mack Carlino had to offer. She didn't care about the voice, and she didn't care about the consequences.

MACK HAD SENSED Teddy's momentary hesitation. He'd felt her struggle with her desire as desperately as he had with his own when he'd lowered her to the rug in front of the fire. But then he had felt the longing that wracked her body as he'd kissed that tantalizing mouth, tasting her desire as distinctly as he could taste the sweet trace of wine on her lips. And when she'd pulled off his shirt, Mack had seen Teddy's passionate longing flickering in her wide eyes.

It was then that Mack had tried to let reason cool the blaze. He'd tried to convince himself that Teddy wasn't his type. It hadn't worked. Then he'd considered Teddy's engagement, however unstable, and reminded himself that he'd been hired by her fiancé. But even *that* thought had done nothing to douse the fire that seared his groin as he held Teddy in his arms, as he felt every inch of her yielding body press against his...ardent, anxious, willing.

And when Mack felt her fingers slide along the waistband of his jeans and linger at the top button, driving him to more exquisite and agonizing anticipation than he'd ever thought possible, Mack *knew* there was no turning back. He'd wanted Teddy from the moment he'd seen her at the bar. No, he'd wanted her even before that—for a week he'd carried her picture in his pocket, and for a week he'd stared into that face, wondering what it might be like...

Never had he thought it could be this powerful.

He heard Teddy's disappointed moan when he slowed their kiss and drew back slightly to prop himself on his elbows. Beneath his chest her breasts pressed against him. And as he covered her body with his, lying between her long, slender legs, Mack had no doubt that Teddy felt his erection, hard and hot against her.

Gazing down into her face, Mack couldn't remember if he'd ever witnessed a more breathtaking vision. Her lips, moist and swollen from their kisses, parted slightly as though she wanted to say something yet found herself as speechless as he was now. But it was Teddy's eyes, those wide cool-gray eyes, that brought Mack's racing heart to a shuddering stop.

She'd been so painfully honest with him tonight, and not only in her desire. Admittedly she'd told him things that she'd not told anyone. And what had he done? Instead of repaying that trust with the truth she deserved, he'd perpetuated the lies that had brought him into her arms.

"I'm sorry, Teddy," he murmured, shaking his head and brushing a wisp of golden hair from her face.

Her eyes widened and her forehead tightened just enough for him to recognize her confusion. "Mack, I—"

"No, please, Teddy." He put a finger to her lips, wishing it was his mouth instead that pressed against the velvety warmth. "I can't do this. I can't take advantage of you."

He could see she was about to protest.

"I *am* just passing through, Teddy. And I don't mean only through Birdseye."

What else could he tell her? The truth? Even with that, he'd be no further ahead. He'd still end up hurting her, and all of a sudden that was the most important thing to Mack— that he not hurt Teddy.

He reached for her T-shirt, and handed it to her as he helped her up from the floor. But she didn't put it on. Instead, Teddy seemed perfectly comfortable with her partial nakedness, standing before him. Or maybe she knew that it was driving him nuts to see her like that, wearing nothing but jeans and that delicate black lace bra, her shimmering blond hair drawn over one shoulder, and her fair skin reflecting the fading glow of the fire.

It took everything Mack had to stop from pulling her into his arms again and satisfying every last fantasy he'd had about Teddy from the moment he'd been handed her photograph.

"Well then, good night, Mack," she said quietly, and he

wished her voice hadn't sounded so cold.

"Good night, Teddy."

She turned. In a few fluid strides, with Bogie at her heels, she crossed the cabin to the bedroom. Long after the door closed, Mack stared after her. When he finally moved to the couch and dropped into the soft cushions, he could smell the faint trace of Teddy's perfume on his skin. He felt the deep, agonizing pull in his groin as he remembered the way her body had yielded to his, the way she'd moved against him, and Mack half wished that the lake outside *would* thaw. He really could use a cold plunge.

"WHERE ARE YOU calling from?" Alan Somerton clutched the office phone even tighter to his ear, struggling to hear through the static of the long-distance line and what sounded like the grating squeal of a transport truck's air brakes.

"From a damned phone booth. Wheredya think?" the husky voice replied.

"Did you find them?"

"Yeah, I think so. Some godforsaken town called Birds- eye. Carlino used a credit card to gas up just the other day."

"So you're going to do it tonight?"

"Cripes! Will ya relax? I gotta locate 'em first, all right?"

"Fine. Fine." Alan lowered himself into the leather chair behind his desk and stared at Teddy's picture. "And you'll make it look like an accident, right?"

"Yeah, sure. An accident. That's what you paid me for, that's what you'll get. I'll call you when it's done."

"Good." Alan dropped the receiver into its cradle. He massaged his throbbing temples. It didn't surprise him that he had a splitting headache. After all, it wasn't every day that one hired a hit man to kill one's fiancée.

8

TEDDY GATHERED the last of her papers from the corner desk and tucked them into the case along with her laptop.

It was time, she thought.

After leaving Mack standing in the middle of the living room last night and closing the bedroom door, she'd gone directly to bed. But she hadn't slept. She'd lain awake for hours, still able to feel Mack's embrace, recalling every place that those seductive hands and those cunning lips had touched her, remembering the way his longing had shifted so quickly from tender and caressing to the same crushing, seemingly insatiable desire that had charged through her own body.

It wasn't until much later in the night that her mind had grasped the significance that one kiss had on her life, and the decisions she had to make. She'd thought about Alan, and Denver, and Logan Publishing. But mostly about Alan and going home.

She'd been gone too long, as it was. Last night was obvious evidence of that. She'd been too quick to give in to her desires, too ready to push aside all reason and answer only her longing to be with Mack.

No. That one kiss, and everything else that it had suggested, had shown Teddy the answer she'd been unable to see before Mack Carlino had entered her life. What she and Alan had—whatever kind of warped relationship it was— was definitely over. After spending almost a year believing that she was going to share her life with Alan Somerton, Teddy should have known that it would take more than a month away to put things in perspective.

It had taken Mack.

It didn't matter that Mack was only passing through her life, that he was leaving today. Her decision didn't have as much to do with Mack as with herself. She had never felt the kind of passion she had last night—not from Alan or any other man in her past—nor had she thought herself capable of the kind of intensity she'd experienced in Mack's arms.

There was no way she could marry Alan now. Not after last night.

The only thing left to do was pack her things, drive back to Denver and tell Alan it was over. Once and for all.

End it.

And the sooner the better.

With Mack leaving, Teddy had no desire to stay in Birdseye. He'd been here for less than two days and already Teddy knew that the cabin would seem empty without him. She doubted she could bear that emptiness.

Besides, she had to get on with her own life. Her own reality. Birdseye, this cabin, and even Mack...they were only fantasy—a fantasy that was rapidly coming to an end.

Teddy looked out the window to the small clearing beyond the end of the porch. Stripped down to his shirt and a fleece vest, Mack picked up another chunk of firewood. He steadied it on the block and raised the ax again. He didn't know she was watching him. Didn't know that she admired the wide outline of his shoulders through the flannel shirt as he swung the ax high and brought it down clear through the log with one powerful blow. She remembered the feel of those shoulders and the strength in those arms.

And as the late-morning sun shimmered off his glossy, black hair, she remembered its thick softness clenched between her fingers when she'd drawn him deeper and deeper into their kiss. She realized then, as she watched Mack and remembered last night, that if he hadn't stopped them...she doubted *she* would have had the willpower.

From the back of the chair, Teddy picked up his sweater. She lifted it to her face and breathed in the too-familiar blend of Mack's after-shave and his own earthy male scent. She was going to miss that smell. *Face it*, she thought as she replaced the sweater. *You're going to miss* him *more.*

The mere thought of his leaving brought an agonizing pain in her chest, a kind of hollowness she'd never felt before. But the reality was, as of this afternoon, Mack would be heading west toward Boise, Idaho, and she would be tossing the last of her things into a suitcase before driving east to Denver. Both forging off in opposite directions, their paths lying miles, and lifetimes, apart.

And it was probably just as well that it ended now...before it had actually begun. Before she actually believed herself to be in love with Mack Carlino.

Even so...if she'd been able to think of a way to convince Mack to stay one more night, Teddy would have tried.

MACK SWUNG the ax considerably harder than he needed to. The piece on the block splintered into several ragged sections that flew across the packed snow. Bogie sat back and watched, keeping his distance as if understanding that the man wielding the ax had more than a little pent-up energy to work out this morning.

Mack looked to the dog. Bogie cocked his massive head, but stayed clear as Mack reached for another chunk of firewood.

Mack had been restless all morning. He'd hardly slept, as it was, on the couch, knowing Teddy was only in the next room, but by seven he'd been too frustrated to just lie there, and had started breakfast. Preparing food had managed to take his mind, at least marginally, off Teddy, but before long she'd stepped through the bedroom door, wrapped in a flannel robe, and the tension had flared anew.

Neither of them dared to mention last night. But who needed to? In the cramped quarters of the kitchen, as Teddy and Mack had tried to settle into some pleasant breakfast chat, the very air around them was positively alive with awareness. And after they'd eaten...it had only gotten worse.

Mack brought the ax down again. The resounding crack echoed through the clearing.

No, it had definitely been worse after breakfast, when they'd tried to clean up. *Tried* being the operative word, he thought. They'd spent more time bumping into each other and apologizing than they had actually spent washing dishes. In the end, Mack had given up. And when he'd told Teddy that he was going to chop firewood, he could have sworn he saw relief on her face, as well. It was driving them both nuts to be that close.

If he didn't leave soon, Mack thought, reaching for another chunk of wood and casting a glance at the cabin, things would *really* get out of hand. Last night had been far too close. Pulling away from her had been the hardest thing he could remember ever having done.

It wasn't just the lies that had made him stop when he'd wanted nothing more than to feel her body move with his, to feel her eager flesh envelop him and to drown in her hot sweetness. No, if it had been only the lies, he would have taken her right there in front of the fire. He would have made love to Teddy all night and not given a damn about the truth—or the consequences.

What he *did* care about was Teddy. It was almost uncharacteristic of him, but no matter how badly he wanted to be with her, he couldn't bear the thought of hurting her. And making love to her last night would have done just that. Once she found out who he was, and who had hired him... She'd never forgive him. And even if, by some miracle, she could find it in her heart to do so, what kind of a future did they have together? Their lives were worlds apart.

Out here, in the paradise of the Rocky Mountain wilderness, they could pretend to be on equal footing. But in reality, in Teddy's reality back in Denver, her life was a world away from all of this, a world away from Mack's.

No, he hadn't been lying when he'd told her he was just "passing through." And it was best that nothing had happened last night. She could pack her things eventually and go back to Denver with a semiclear conscience. Back into Alan's waiting arms. After all, she *was* still engaged to the man. Where did Mack get off even contemplating a life with another man's future bride?

He had to be insane. No. Being around Teddy Logan *made* him insane, he realized as he swung the ax even higher.

Maybe he should head back to Denver right now. He'd wanted to know Teddy's side of the story, and he'd gotten it. He'd questioned her about Alan Somerton, and as far as Mack could tell, maybe it *had* been a lovers' quarrel that had brought Teddy here. There was no reason why he shouldn't just march straight into Somerton's office at Logan Publishing and tell him where Teddy was. Get the rest of his money and be done with it.

But Mack couldn't imagine doing that. He couldn't betray Teddy, no matter how badly his business needed the money.

And maybe Blake would actually find something dirty in Somerton's past, something that would convince Teddy to leave the guy. *But then what?* he asked himself as he buried the head of the ax in the chopping block. Did he honestly believe that she'd come rushing into his arms after all those lies?

Blake was right. He should never have gotten involved. Sure, this was different from two years ago. No one's life was at risk. But he'd still allowed himself to become personally involved. He'd still messed up.

He looked around him now, seeing the destruction his restlessness had wrecked on the woodpile, and started to scoop up the chopped firewood. It was then that Mack noticed Bogie at the edge of the clearing. The malamute's nose was buried in the snow, his large tail fanning the air excitedly.

"Bogie. Come on, boy."

The dog refused to look up. Mack dropped the armload of wood and waded through the snow toward him.

"This had better be good, Bogie," Mack told him as he felt the snow jam into the tops of his boots. And when he finally made it across the small clearing, Mack saw what the malamute found so fascinating.

Tracks. A single trail of boot prints in the knee-deep snow ran from the edge of the clearing, through the low trees, and, Mack was certain, to the bordering road. And they appeared relatively fresh. There had been snow early last night, not much, but enough that it should have at least softened the edges of the deep tracks if they'd been made earlier.

Bogie tilted his head toward Mack, as if awaiting instructions. Mack reached down and stroked the dog pensively for a moment, and was about to step into the woods to follow the trail when he heard the four-wheel drive pull up to the cabin. Bogie was through the clearing and bounding toward the truck even before Sly could wave a hand to Mack.

The old man stepped around the hood of his vehicle,

waited at the edge of the driveway, and crossed his arms over his barrel chest.

"Those must be some shoulders you have there," he said, nodding to the woodpile. "Guess I won't be having to come up here for a good week now, huh?"

Mack pushed through the deep snow to the woodblock, stopping in the clearing to brush off his jeans. "Don't be so sure, Sly," he said. "I think Teddy will want the company."

"Oh, yeah? And how do you figure that? Are you leaving?"

"I'm heading out right after we pick up the Jeep."

Sly's nod was almost solemn, and Mack was surprised not to see any satisfaction on the man's face. Perhaps Sly Valeriano was warming up to him, after all.

"Listen, Sly, what do you make of tracks up in these parts?"

"Tracks?" Sly scratched his chin beneath the heavy white beard. "What kind o' tracks?"

"Boot prints. Running from the clearing to the road."

"Not Teddy's?"

"No. I'd say they were from this morning."

"Probably poachers."

"Poachers? This close to the cabin?"

"Yeah, I suppose it's possible. They trap up here. Not supposed to, but they do. You might wanna keep an eye on Bogie here." He chuckled and gave the dog's back a quick rub. "Wouldn't want someone thinking they'd found themselves a wolf. Or, by the size o' him, a bear."

Sly turned from him when the cabin door swung open, and Mack followed the man's smiling gaze.

Teddy.

Almost immediately Mack felt the familiar pull in his groin—it was becoming an automatic reaction anytime he laid eyes on her.

She hadn't bothered with a coat, and instead wrapped her arms around herself as she came down the steps and into sunshine. It wouldn't have mattered though, Mack thought. Whether Teddy was wearing the shirt and jeans or five parkas and a dozen scarves, he'd still be able to imagine the lithe, sensuous body that moved beneath those clothes.

He watched her approach, and when she met his gaze he knew she harbored the same thoughts he did. Mack turned to the wood.

"So I see you've gone and found yourself someone who's handier with that old ax than I am," Sly was saying as he slipped an arm over her shoulders and walked her to the porch.

Mack watched them from the corner of his eye while he stacked the wood. He couldn't make out her words, but he saw Teddy pace as she spoke. With her hands buried in the front pockets of her jeans, she kicked at a piece of ice that had fallen from the roof. She looked serious. So did Sly. And then Mack watched as Teddy put her arms around Sly and hugged him.

When they parted, Mack saw her give Sly one of those soft, glowing smiles that he'd come to love, the kind that made him long to feel that easy curve against his own lips.

"Mack?" Teddy waved him over as she walked Sly to his truck.

Dropping an armload of wood onto the already waist-high pile, he joined them. And even with the hood of Sly's truck separating him from Teddy, Mack wondered if he'd ever be able to look at the woman again without feeling the deep shudders of desire that whipped through him now.

"Mack, I'm having Sly and Maryanne and her husband, Rick, over for dinner tonight. Nothing fancy. But I...I'd like you to stay. I mean, if you can. After everything you've done, dinner is the least I can offer."

Her quick smile and the way she nervously pulled her hair over one shoulder before jamming her hands into her jeans pockets convinced Mack that the implication of her last sentence was wholly unintended.

"Of course," she added, "I'd certainly understand if you—"

"No, I can stay...for dinner."

But Mack knew why Teddy had asked him in front of Sly. With Sly there, Mack wouldn't argue. He'd be more likely to say yes to her invitation, and wouldn't dare breathe a word of the danger in his staying a few more minutes, let alone a few more hours.

"SO WHERE *did* you learn to cook like that?" Maryanne stood at the kitchen sink, elbow-deep in suds, and handed Teddy another plate.

"Actually," Teddy admitted as she dried the plate and glanced to where Mack was embroiled in conversation with Rick and Sly by the fire, "I'm usually all thumbs in the kitchen. I mean, it's not like I never cook for myself, but it's been a while since I've cooked for others. So I confess, Mack helped a little."

"Hmm...so he cooks, as well, huh?"

"Maryanne—" But Teddy's warning was unheeded.

"Well, are you going to fill me in? I thought you told me 'one night.' Something about doctor's orders?"

Teddy saw the mischief in Maryanne's eyes, and knew she couldn't answer the question truthfully. Besides, how could she possibly put into words the overwhelming feelings she had for Mack? Or the longing that locked her breath in her throat and sent that low, burning ache through her body even as she looked at him now, across the cabin. In one hand he cradled his wineglass, his fingers cupped around its bowl in the same gentle curve that he'd held her breast last night. And when he caught her staring at him, a smile softened his firm lips and Teddy once again felt that familiar swell within her.

The afternoon hadn't been easy. After Sly left, Mack had finished with the wood, taken a shower and brushed the snow off the Mustang. The drive to Birdseye had been quiet. After stopping for a few groceries and other necessities, they'd picked up Teddy's car from the garage. Then Teddy had followed in her Jeep as Mack led the way up to the cabin.

And by the time they'd managed to get dinner under control, as well as themselves, Teddy had been almost grateful for Maryanne's arrival with the guys.

"Well, I know why he's sticking around," Maryanne said, no longer waiting for an answer.

"And what's your theory?" Teddy asked, hoping their voices couldn't be heard in the living room.

"The man's in love with you."

"Maryanne, I hardly think that in two days—"

"Oh, come on, Teddy. What? Are you completely blind? Check out the way he looks at you. Heck, Rick, my own husband, sweet man that he is, doesn't look at me like *that*."

As if on cue, Mack caught Teddy's stare again. Even across the distance of the cabin, she could see the provocative intimacy that swam in his eyes.

"So, do you want to tell me about that engagement ring of yours? And don't go telling me that it was fake and you only wore it to keep the guys off you at the bar. Cuz, honey, that was no fake diamond. I may be just a hick from Birdseye, Colorado, but I *know* the real thing when I see it."

"It's a long story, Maryanne."

"So what are you saying? You're not engaged?"

"What I'm saying," Teddy told her, handing Maryanne the towel, "is that it's a long story."

The other woman dried her hands, studied Teddy briefly and seemed to resign herself at last. But Teddy knew that the final word was always Maryanne's.

"Well," Maryanne added in a low whisper as she started to leave the kitchen, "I don't care *how* rich or good-looking the other guy is, I know one thing—he can't have anything on Mack. You did right to lose the ring, honey."

Teddy was still shaking her head when Maryanne reached for the coats and turned to Sly and Rick. "Come on, boys. It's time I got you home. Say your goodbyes and let's get." And in another aside to Teddy, she added, "I wouldn't dream of cutting in on any of your evening plans."

MACK AND TEDDY waved goodbye from the doorway, standing together as the big truck lumbered down the driveway to the road. And even once the headlights were no longer visible through the heavy snowfall, the two of them remained there for a long moment, as though the cold air could offer a margin of lucidity.

It was Teddy who headed inside first. Mack closed the door and joined her, collecting wineglasses and the empty bottle from the living room and taking them to the kitchen.

Sly had already warned them about the predicted snow-fall, and it had been an unspoken understanding that Mack would stay one more night. One more night on the couch, he thought as he dried the glass Teddy handed him.

He could make it. He'd have to.

"You have good friends in Sly and Maryanne," he told Teddy, hoping that small talk would ease the tension that sparked the air between them. "They really care about you."

"I know they do. They're good people. I'm going to miss them."

"So...you're going home then? To Denver?"

"Of course I'm going back to Denver, Mack. I can't hide out here forever, as much as I'd like to." There was a sharpness in her voice, a hint of resentment. "I'm going to leave in the morning. I already told Sly."

Mack remembered the hug he'd seen them share on the front porch this morning. He should have guessed something was up. But he hadn't expected Teddy to be returning to Denver so soon. He wondered it if was because of him.

This changed things, he thought, quickly weighing this latest development. If Teddy was leaving in the morning, then his assignment was over. He'd not betrayed her. He'd not "turned her in" to Alan Somerton. And he'd not screwed up. Not really.

On the other hand, it also meant that this was it. As of tomorrow, both he and Teddy returned to their own lives, their own realities. It was over.

"I've got to face the music," she said as she washed the last glass. "There's work to be done at Logan Publishing. I can't put it off any longer."

Mack noticed how she'd failed to mention Alan Somerton in her plans.

"So, in the morning, huh?"

Teddy nodded. "I have most of my stuff already packed. I promised Sly that I'd stop by the bar to return his keys. And write him a check for the Jeep."

"No more hiding?"

"No more hiding," she echoed, and gave him an almost defeated smile.

"You know," he said, "I could..."

"What?"

"Actually, no. Forget it. It's nothing."

"What is it, Mack?" She turned to him, leaning her hip against the counter as she dried her hands.

Why was it that he couldn't even meet Teddy's gaze without the sudden urge to sweep her into his arms? Mack looked to the window above the sink, but there was only the black emptiness of the night...and Teddy's perfect reflection in the glass, her face tilted up to his, staring expectantly.

Mack bit down on the urge and looked at her. "I was just thinking that...I could drive with you into Birdseye." But what he'd really wanted to suggest was that he drive her to Denver. The only trouble was, he couldn't think of any plausible explanation for doing so. *He* was supposed to be heading to his brother's in Boise, Idaho, as far as Teddy was concerned.

"Maybe we could have lunch or something. Then again, you probably want to hit the road early."

"No," she said, setting down the towel. "No, lunch would be good."

"Great."

It was at that moment, when Teddy stepped away from the counter and handed Mack the last glass, that the night exploded. A single gunshot shattered the window and ripped through the silence of the cabin.

And in the same instant, Mack hit the floor.

9

IT ALL HAPPENED so fast. One second Teddy had been staring into Mack's smile, and the next she was on the kitchen floor.

Everything had been a blur—first the ear-splitting crack, then Mack's body colliding with hers, forcing her down, and finally, his weight on top of her.

By the time Teddy opened her eyes, the kitchen was in total darkness.

"Mack! Mack, what happened?"

He was motionless, the length of his body covering hers.

A gunshot. That's what it had been. She was sure of it. Teddy's mind staggered with the awful truth. Mack had been shot!

"Mack?" Her hands shook when she clutched at his shoulders, pushing him back, trying to see his face. "Mack!"

"Shh."

"You're...you're all right?"

"Yeah, I'm fine." His whisper cut through the silence, and she felt him shift above her. "Just stay down, Teddy."

"What was it? A gunshot?"

A thin shaft of light from the living room caught the side of Mack's face as he eased himself up. She was sure he nodded.

"Are you all right, Teddy?"

"Yeah, I think so."

His hands were on her now. Strong fingers sweeping over

her chest and torso, but there was a desperation, a quiet panic, in Mack's touch. And Teddy realized what he was doing. He thought she'd been shot.

"Mack."

Still he continued to check her, as though having to assure himself that she was not hurt.

"Mack!" Her whisper was harsh enough to stop him at last. "Mack. I'm fine."

"You're sure?"

"Yes. I'm sure. Just tell me what's going on. What—"

"I don't know. It was probably a stray bullet. Poachers maybe." But it didn't sound as though Mack put much faith in his theory.

"What happened to the lights?"

"I turned them off," he answered, and Teddy realized how quickly Mack had reacted. He must have hit the bank of light switches at the side of the counter even as he had dragged her to the floor.

With Mack still straddling her, Teddy propped herself up onto her elbows. She felt his hand, broad and warm, against her cheek.

"Look, Teddy, you have to stay put, you hear me?" He started to shift away from her.

"No way. I'm not—"

He pressed his index finger to her lips. "I mean it, Teddy. Just stay here. And don't move."

She nodded, and then he was gone. She heard him cross the kitchen, watched his low shadow as he crept through the living room. He whispered a command to Bogie, and when she saw Mack again, he was crouching over his duffel bag by the sofa. Seconds later the entire cabin fell into utter darkness as he switched off the last lamp.

"Mack?"

"It's all right, Teddy." He was close again. Crouching a

few feet from her, she realized, in the doorway. She started to move toward him. "No. Just stay there."

"What are you doing?"

"I'm going outside—"

"Mack, don't be crazy!"

"I have to check this out."

"No. We should call someone. Get the authorities. You can't—" And then she heard the distinct slide of metal against metal, a cold, harsh sound that sent a chill through her—Mack's gun.

"Mack."

He was beside her again, pressing his palm against her cheek. "Teddy, it's okay. I'll be right back." He tried to calm her, but the kiss he placed on her lips to silence her protest had an unsettling urgency about it. "Just promise me you'll stay here," he whispered.

When she reached out for him, her hand found only empty air. His shadow flitted briefly in the hallway, and he was gone.

She didn't hear the latch on the cabin door, but she felt the brief draft of cold air when Mack opened and closed it. Then, a heavy silence.

She listened, half expecting to hear another gunshot rip through the night. There was only the deafening pounding of her heart.

Seconds swelled into minutes. Teddy's mind raced. What if it wasn't a poacher? What if someone was after Mack? He was a cop; even if he was on leave, it wasn't illogical to think he might have a few enemies. Or maybe there was a lot more to Mack Carlino than she was aware of. Maybe there were things about him he hadn't told her. After all, how could you possibly know someone after only two days?

From the living room, Bogie let out a soft, nervous whimper. Teddy released the breath she'd been holding. Following the line of cupboards, she crawled to the hallway. Bogie whined again. In the pallid moonlight that slipped through the windows, she saw a flash of white and silver fur, and in moments Bogie was at her side. She threw an arm around him, grateful for his presence.

It was then that Teddy noticed the blood.

She mustn't have been aware of it in her panic. But now, as she angled her hand in a faint shaft of moonlight and felt the warm stickiness on her palm, the sight of the dark smear shocked her.

But whose blood was it? Could there have been glass on the floor from the broken window? Had she cut herself? With another wave of panic forcing her heart into her throat, Teddy checked herself over.

No. She was fine.

It was Mack. Mack's blood on her hands. He *had* been shot!

"Damn you, Mack," she swore under her breath and got to her feet. She was still cursing him when her hand closed around the knob of the front door. She cursed him for lying to her, for making her believe he was uninjured, and she cursed him for rushing off into the night like some vigilante.

IT WAS SNOWING harder now, and in the deathly silent night, Teddy was sure she could hear each flake strike the ground.

Clouds loomed above, skulking across the charcoal sky like great beasts devouring the three-quarter moon. She had never imagined a night could be so black.

She wiped snow from her face and eyes. Her hands were shaking even more than before. Shaking from the cold and from her anger. How could Mack just race out here in the middle of the night, shot and bleeding, to face God-knows-what?

"Mack?" she whispered.

Nothing.

After slinking off the front porch and creeping along the perimeter of the cabin, she'd whispered his name several times. Not once had it elicited a response.

She shivered and pressed herself back against the rough logs. She gulped in another lungful of freezing air and held it, listening for any sound that might lead her to him.

Still nothing. Only a short burst of wind rattling through the branches.

"Mack!"

What if he'd gone into the woods? What then? What if he'd seen something and taken off in pursuit? And then collapsed from his injury. Or worse... She'd never find him there.

Teddy edged closer to the cabin's corner. Her heart rammed against her ribs, and her mind reeled as she again felt the stickiness along her palm.

Mack was hurt.

One more step took her to the end of the wall. Her hands clenched into tight fists. Every muscle in her body quivered as fear tightened around her chest. She could hardly breathe. In her mind, she'd already imagined the worst; imagined finding Mack bleeding to death in some snowdrift.

But when she inched around the corner and peered through the blackness, she let out a brief sigh of relief. The clearing was empty.

"Mack," she whispered his name again, biting back the last traces of anger as fear rapidly took over. "Dammit, Mack. Where are you?"

Perhaps she'd made a mistake coming out here. Maybe she *should* have called the police.

"Mack, please," she pleaded into the empty darkness.

And she was about to turn, to head back inside, when she

felt a sudden flurry of movement in the air around her. Teddy spun around. But she was too late.

One broad hand clamped over her mouth, trapping a scream. And before she could twist herself free of her attacker, an arm locked around her chest. Iron-hard muscles constricted ever tighter as she struggled against him. She tried to wrest herself from his grip, desperately jerking her head back and forth, but the hand over her mouth was like a vise.

In seconds, he turned with her, pinning her between the rough logs of the cabin and his own solidness. Feeling him rigid against her and his breath hot against her temple, Teddy recognized the powerful body that held her captive an instant before he whispered in her ear.

"Shh. Teddy, it's all right."

He relaxed his hold on her, easing his hand from her mouth.

Teddy turned within Mack's arms, and felt herself dissolve into his embrace.

"Mack. Mack, my God, where—"

"Shh. Listen."

Even Mack was holding his breath now. Standing in each other's arms, they listened to the night. The clouds overhead parted briefly and moonlight once again spilled across the blanket of snow around them.

"I thought I heard something."

Teddy heard it then, too. The muffled rumble of a car's engine starting up, out on the road somewhere, beyond the woods. Within seconds the sound faded and was gone.

"I thought I told you to stay put." Mack held her at arm's length at last. He lifted a hand to brush the snow from her hair.

But Teddy ignored him. Her hands skimmed across his shirt, searching for his injury.

"Teddy? What's the matter?"

Perhaps it was her anger at Mack's foolish heroics, or the dreadful scenarios that had been running through her mind, but Teddy couldn't speak. As her fingers fluttered across his chest, she tried to convince herself that he was fine. He was standing before her, after all. He *had* to be all right.

And finally, Mack snatched her wrists. "Teddy? What is it?"

She tore her hand free and held it up so he could see it. "Blood, Mack! And it's not mine. You've been shot."

Then she saw his shirt.

"It's a flesh wound, Teddy. I'm fine. It's nothing."

"Like hell it's nothing. Look at your sleeve." The stain had spread across his shoulder, soaking into the soft flannel. It glistened darkly in the moonlight.

ONCE INSIDE, Mack stumbled through the cabin, closing all the shutters. He didn't offer her any explanation, but then Teddy hadn't asked for one. She'd gone directly to the medicine chest in the tiny bathroom, tossing aside bottles of aspirin and antihistamines along with numerous brands of flu remedies, but found nothing resembling first-aid supplies.

In the sterile light of the vanity bulb, the sight of Mack's blood on her hands was even more shocking than before. Maybe it was only a flesh wound as Mack suggested, but it could have been worse. Much worse.

Teddy washed her hands, trying to stop their shaking as she watched the last of the blood swirl down the drain.

She was already wetting a cloth and taking a fresh towel from the drawer when Mack came up behind her.

"Teddy." His voice was barely a whisper, and still she practically jumped out of her skin at the sound of it.

He stood in the doorway, filling it with his broad shoulders. In his right hand he held his leather duffel bag. The shoulder of his gray flannel shirt was stained a deep crimson, and she could see the tattered edges of the tear that the bullet had made.

"I've got some first-aid stuff in my bag," he offered. "Why don't you just leave me to it?"

"No way, Mack." She shook her head and wrested the duffel bag from his grasp. "I'm going to look at that shoulder myself. *I'll* be the one to decide whether or not you need a doctor."

She ushered him out of the cramped bathroom and over to the side of the bed. "Now, sit," she ordered, reaching for the bedside lamp and dropping the bag onto the blanket.

"Teddy, I think I can manage this."

"Humor me, Mack, all right?" She sat next to him and angled the lamp toward his shoulder.

He complied, taking out gauze and antiseptic from the bag, and at last unbuttoning his shirt. When she brushed the shirt over his broad shoulders and started to wipe carefully at the drying blood, Teddy saw him fight back a grimace. And when she dabbed around the small gash barely an inch above his left bicep, she heard his sharp intake of breath.

But Mack remained silent. Letting her work.

The bleeding had stopped, and seeing the wound now, Teddy realized he was right. It didn't require medical attention. It was just a flesh wound. But one or two inches over, she realized, and he would not have been so lucky.

The thought settled coldly in her heart, sending an involuntary shiver through her as she unwound a section of gauze.

"I think we should call the sheriff," she told him, her voice stronger now, her hands steadier as she cut the gauze.

"It's late, Teddy. This isn't the city. You realize you'd be getting the sheriff out of bed right about now?"

"I don't care. Somebody just tried to shoot you, Mack."

"Don't be crazy. It was probably some poachers."

"Crazy? 'Crazy' is running out into the dead of night without having a clue what's out there."

"I'm all right, aren't I?"

"You could have been killed, Mack." Her voice started to waver again.

He must have heard it, as well, because he reached over and placed his hand on her thigh. Teddy ripped a piece of tape off the roll and tried to ignore the heat that surged through her from his mere touch.

He kept his hand there for a long while, watching her patch his shoulder, letting the silence grow between them. Only when she'd finished did Teddy dare to meet his gaze again.

"Are you in some kind of trouble, Mack?"

"No, Teddy, I'm not."

"Because if you are, well, maybe there's something I can do to help. I don't know what exactly, but—"

"Teddy—" he grasped her shoulders and shifted on the edge of the bed so that he faced her "—Teddy, trust me, I'm not in any trouble. No one is after me. It was only a stray bullet."

But she saw the trace of disquiet that flickered across his face. He leaned toward her, holding her steady gaze as he lifted one hand from her shoulder to cradle her face.

She'd experienced those lips before. She *knew* the kind of magic they were capable of. She should have been prepared for it, but still Mack's kiss left her breathless. With beguiling skill, his lips parted hers, and Teddy drank in his tender kiss, wondering why it didn't feel wrong this time.

Under her palm, she felt the subtle shift of muscle across Mack's bare chest as he drew closer, and then his heartbeat—rapid and strong as her own.

She lifted her hands to his neck and pulled him to her,

wanting him to feel the urgency that raced through her, wishing that it would never end. Yet the thought had barely flitted through her mind when he drew back. His fingers fanned through her hair, and he toyed with one strand as Teddy felt his breath whisper across her lips.

With his forehead resting against hers, he was so close she could feel his mouth form the words: "Teddy, I...I really think you should get some sleep."

But there was a dark frustration in Mack's voice. Teddy knew he longed for the same thing she did, yet he refused to surrender to that longing.

Without another word, he stood up. It was then that Teddy realized she could not let Mack go. She couldn't be without him tonight. She couldn't lie in this bed alone, knowing that he was in the other room...and that he wouldn't be there tomorrow.

She caught his hand in hers, and when Mack looked down to meet her stare, she wondered what she could possibly say to make him stay. All she knew was that if he left her now, she would shatter. Never had she wanted anything more than she wanted to be with Mack tonight.

"Please, Mack." She tried to control the tremble in her voice. "Don't go."

"Teddy, I—"

"No. Listen to me, Mack. I...I don't care if you're only passing through my life." She caressed his hand, lowering her gaze to his wide knuckles and strong fingers, unable to look him in the eye for fear that he might see the tears she struggled to hold back.

"Even if we have only tonight, only this once, I...I want to be with you, Mack," she confessed at last.

He was silent for a long time, until finally Teddy was certain that he would say something horribly pragmatic—tell her how they shouldn't, how they couldn't, how they had separate paths, lives that could never come together.

Instead, Mack lowered himself to the bed. He placed a finger under her chin and tilted her face so that she was forced to look at him. And as she gazed into his handsome face, into the eyes she knew she could never forget as long as she lived, Teddy wished the circumstances were different, that she might have met Mack at another time in her life, when their paths didn't lie in opposite directions and when she might have had the luxury of falling in love with him. Because there was little doubt in her mind, as he held her stare, that she *could* fall in love with Mack Carlino.

"Teddy." His voice was as gentle as the finger that traced the line of her lips. "Are you sure?"

"I don't think I've ever been more sure of anything in my entire life." When she reached out to him, she knew that he felt her hand tremble. "Make love to me, Mack."

In one fluid motion, his strong arms circled her waist, and he eased her back on the bed. His mouth was on hers again, answering her thirst with a kiss so passionate, so deep and earnest, that Teddy knew there was no turning back.

This was where she wanted to be. This was what she'd imagined. Nothing existed beyond the walls of the cabin; nothing mattered except the man in her arms and their intimate union.

Mack shifted his weight, straddling her, his thighs tight against her hips. When he drew back to gaze down at her, the trepidation she'd seen in his face only moments ago was replaced by a small smile. She reached up, feeling the heat of their kiss on his lips.

From there, she traced the line of his jaw, and as he straightened up, her fingers skimmed across the soft mat of hair on his chest and down his torso, feeling each muscle quiver in response to her touch. Reaching behind him, Mack withdrew the semiautomatic from the waistband of his jeans and placed it on the nightstand. The sight of the gun was a cold reminder of what had happened tonight. Of what *could* have happened. And thinking about how close Mack had come to losing his life, Teddy needed him even more desperately.

She wanted him to rip the clothes from her body and consume her totally, to drive her to heights she'd only dreamed of, to drown her in the madness of their lovemaking.

Instead, Mack reached down and unfastened each button of her shirt, one by one, with such unrelenting patience she thought she'd go mad. He tugged the ends of the shirt free from her jeans and slowly brushed back the sides. He trailed his fingertips across her belly, sending shivers spiraling downward. Then up to her chest, where he traced a finger along the outline of her bra before cupping one breast in each strong hand. With his thumbs he circled her nipples, and finally unclasped the bra and pulled back the lace. And when he lowered his mouth over one nipple and then the other, sucking and teasing each one in turn, Teddy thought she might explode with desire.

She writhed beneath him, but her hips were locked securely between his thighs. She reached down, dragging her fingers through his thick hair, and pulled him toward her, needing to feel that magical mouth devour hers.

When she opened her eyes again, Mack leaned over her. The devilish smile that played on his lips was evidence that he recognized her impatience. He brushed a wisp of hair from her face, and came closer, nuzzling his lips against her ear.

"We have all night, Teddy," he told her, his hoarse whisper sending a sweet shudder through her.

His mouth was hot against her neck, his tongue even hotter, as his kisses burned steadily downward, past her throat, her shoulders, between her breasts and along her stomach. He shifted over her, fanning his hands across her rib cage and sliding them to her waist, lifting her slightly as his lips blazed along her stomach. And when his fingers toyed with the button on her jeans, Teddy raised her hips toward him, almost frantic with anticipation.

Still, Mack flirted with patience. Slowly he undid the button and finally her zipper. And as he pulled back the denim edges, he slid one finger along the waistband of her panties. His kisses followed, trailing feverishly from her hips, across her belly and unmercifully lower, until Teddy could no longer remain quiet.

"Mack." His name came from somewhere deep in her throat. When she called his name a second time, he shifted above her again, bringing his mouth over hers and catching her moan with one of his own. The kiss he gave her this time was firmer, more demanding, and when his body covered hers, Teddy wasn't surprised to feel his erection straining against the thick denim of his jeans, pressing along her belly.

She wanted to feel him. Wanted to reach down and wrap her fingers around him, to feel the intensity of his arousal. But at that same moment, as though sensing her impatience, and determined to keep her on the brink he'd already taken her to, Mack lifted her hips.

Breathlessly, Teddy arched against him. His hand glided between their hot bodies, down past her stomach and under her panties. She was liquid fire long before his fingers found her damp heat and began their delicious stroking. With his mouth still clamped over hers, Teddy couldn't determine where one sensation began and the other ended. The rhythm of Mack's tongue in complete sync with his skillful fingers drove Teddy over that edge on which he'd kept her for so long.

She slid her hands up his strong back to his shoulders, feeling the sheer power in his body, and the incredible restraint locked in each rippling muscle. And as she thrust her hips against his hand, his probing deeper and ever sweeter, Teddy gripped the covers in her fists and climaxed.

When Mack kissed her again, it was slow and gentle. Calming. But she knew he was far from finished. No, she was certain that Mack was just beginning to warm up.

She shared his smile when he looked down at her, wishing she could find the words to express the passion she had for him, for someone who had so selflessly taken her to a place she'd never imagined possible. But if she *had* found the words, Teddy wouldn't have had the opportunity to speak them—Mack was already moving his hands over her body yet again.

Even before she'd managed to catch her breath, Teddy felt him tug at her jeans and remove them completely. But this time, as Mack shifted above her, Teddy was faster. She slid her hand along his torso and to the waistband of his jeans. It was Mack's turn to groan, and the sound of it made Teddy smile as she ran her hand over the stiff denim, caressing the length of his erection.

Now *she* was in control. In one graceful movement, she slid out from under Mack, turned him and straddled his hips.

A low chuckle rose from Mack's throat. "Okay," he said simply with a you-got-me smile on his face.

She smiled back, discarding her shirt and bra, amazed at how comfortable she was in her nakedness before him. In the soft amber light of the bedside lamp, she studied the perfect lines of his face and the magnificent contours of his body, tracing each one with her fingertips. No matter what happened after tonight, she wanted to commit every detail of Mack to memory.

Lowering her lips to his hot skin, Teddy dropped kisses along his shoulders, then his chest and torso, administering the same tantalizing treatment that Mack had lavished on her. He tasted faintly of salt, and his own earthy male scent filled her senses, driving her desire so close to that familiar brink that by the time Teddy reached the waistband of his jeans, she could barely contain her own anticipation.

Unzipping his pants, she slid her hand inside, beneath the thick denim, beneath the waistband of his boxer shorts, and heard the small gasp that whispered from her throat. She'd known Mack was ready, had felt his erection hard against her thigh only a moment ago, but she hadn't expected his size. A fiery hunger surged through her now as she wrapped her fingers around his flesh.

"Oh, Teddy." The sound of her name, spoken in a voice so thick with hunger, sent another wave of desire straight to her core.

Mack raised himself onto his elbows to meet her kiss, and Teddy felt a moan start deep in his chest and finally erupt from his throat and into her own mouth as she stroked his straining shaft.

"Teddy." He was almost breathless, and when she looked into his eyes, she swore she saw her own longing mirrored there.

"Teddy, if we do this, I...I doubt I'll be able to stop."

She didn't let up, but instead gave him a slow smile. "And why on earth would I want you to stop?"

Mack let out a long sigh and fell back onto the tangled covers. But not for long. With great and sudden agility, he rolled over and straddled Teddy once again. Feeling the strength of his body rising above her, Teddy already anticipated feeling the full length of him buried deep within her. But she waited as Mack rummaged through his duffel bag on the floor. She might have asked him if he always kept a stash of comdoms in that bag, or if he'd picked them up at the drugstore in Birdseye this afternoon. Right now though, Teddy didn't care.

When Mack lowered his body to hers, she was amazed at how every angle fit so perfectly into her curves. He kissed her, his hands again working their magic as he touched every part of her, and when at last his lips left hers and she met his steady gaze, Teddy was surprised by the concern behind his dark eyes.

"No regrets?" he asked.

She pressed a palm to his cheek. "Not a one."

No, she thought as she welcomed his smile, her sole regret was that they had only this one night. But better that than never having felt this kind of driving passion. And Teddy was almost certain she could survive a lifetime on the memories of this one night alone, memories of her time with Mack.

Bracing himself over her, Mack at long last entered her. But not in the way that she'd ever experienced before. Instead of the usual headlong rush, Mack moved inside of her slowly, teasingly. Little by little he filled her, each gentle thrust exhilaratingly unique, until eventually he was engulfed within her. With his entire body encompassing hers, he nuzzled her ear.

"Oh, Teddy," he confessed, his voice low and ragged, "you can't imagine how I've dreamed of this. You and me..."

His thrusts then were painfully slow and exquisitely deep, and she met each one eagerly, lifting her hips to the same rhythm. It was as if they'd both been here already, she thought, a thousand times, in their fantasies. And yet, even in her wildest dreams, she could never have prepared herself for Mack's lovemaking. Never had she hovered on the brink of release for as long as he kept her there. She hadn't thought it humanly possible.

"Mack," she whispered his name. Somewhere between delirium and desperation, she pleaded with him to take her at last. With his thrusts venturing deeper, and every muscle in his body straining as he drove into her with increasing urgency, Teddy felt his body go rigid.

And when her own white-hot release wracked her body, she heard Mack call out her name. In all her life, Teddy couldn't recall ever hearing a more honest sound.

10

MACK DIDN'T JOLT awake as he normally did in strange places. Nor was there that instant of disorientation—that frantic moment of piecing together the previous night's events in a desperate effort to figure out how he came to be in a bed other than his own.

This morning, Mack knew exactly where he was. Even before he opened his eyes.

The slow rhythm of Teddy's breathing, her soft hair tickling his shoulder, her breath fanning across his chest and the feel of her lithe body tucked against his as though they were two pieces of a whole...these were the sensations that had stayed with Mack throughout the night. Those, and the all-too-clear memories of what they had shared.

With his eyes still shut against the harsh reality of morning, Mack clung to those exquisite memories, savoring them as he had savored Teddy last night. As they'd savored each other.

None of his fantasies about Teddy had come anywhere close to what he'd experienced with her, and all the daydreams in the world could not have prepared him for the passion he'd found in her arms. Never before had he been filled with such unimaginably sweet contentment and at the same time been wracked by that seemingly unquenchable, agonizing thirst for more.

But it wasn't just him. Last night he'd recognized the longing that had driven Teddy into his arms, the power of her desire bringing her to him again and again. They had *both* been conscious of the fact that they had one night and one night only. They had both wished it could last forever and knew it couldn't, but neither was able to deny the passion that drove them to the edge and always took them over with such breathless exhilaration.

In his mind, Mack could still hear Teddy's low voice, her utter rapture, when she'd pleaded for him to take her. He couldn't recall the sound of his name ever moving him the way it had last night when it had come from her lips.

Mack took in a deep breath. The scent of their lovemaking and the intoxicating fragrance that was intrinsically Teddy filled his senses, stirring that insatiable longing within him.

One night. It had been so much, and yet it seemed as though they had only *begun* to explore the possibilities within one another.

Teddy stirred next to him, but didn't wake. She nuzzled her body closer against his, finding a fit even more perfect than before, and drew her arm tighter around him.

When he opened his eyes at last, the first thing Mack saw was that fair-skinned arm across his tanned chest—a contrast as distinct as night and day.

But then, wasn't that what they were? Their lives revolved in completely separate worlds. Teddy's background, her life-style, even her needs and her dreams, lay in a realm beyond anything Mack was capable of providing. Who was he kidding? Teddy belonged with a man like Alan Somerton, someone who had that corporate sense, that high-finance mentality.

The cold reality of it was, Mack would never stand a chance in Teddy's world.

Nor would she ever fit into his. So there was no sense in dreaming.

And hell, that wasn't even the worst of it, Mack thought,

turning his head so he could look at Teddy's peaceful face. He lifted a hand to brush a blond wisp from her cheek. No, the worst of it was the lies. The lies, and Alan Somerton.

Mack restrained a cynical laugh as he thought about his client. The irony of this situation was that if it *hadn't* been for Alan Somerton, he and Teddy would never have met, they would never have shared this once-in-a-lifetime passion. And yet it was *because* of Alan Somerton that their time was destined to end.

Mack reached over and trailed his hand along her cool skin, past her shoulder and over her delicate rib cage, to the familiar curve of her small waist where he snatched the edge of the covers and pulled them carefully over her.

He watched her sleep. Maybe it was the way the morning sun fingered through the slats of the shutters and touched her golden hair, or maybe it was the way that, even in sleep, a soft smile turned up the corners of that luscious mouth, but Mack couldn't help thinking she had an innocence about her. And he wondered...no, he *prayed* that when Teddy returned to Denver and to Alan, that she would not be wracked with guilt over what they had shared last night.

Mack was glad he had made Teddy happy, if only for one night. He'd enjoyed watching her come apart for him, again and again. He'd delighted in seeing her pleasure and knowing that he was the one who made her feel so fulfilled. And he'd hate to think of any guilt darkening the memory of their one time together.

Mack eased himself from under Teddy's arm and pulled the covers over her shoulder as he stood up from the bed.

She told him that she'd have no regrets. But still, Mack couldn't help wondering if that would be true for her. Because it certainly wasn't true for him.

He *did* have regrets.

He regretted that he'd discovered feelings beyond anything he'd even thought possible, and that the one person he wanted to tell most—the person with whom he was falling in love—he could say nothing to. He couldn't burden Teddy with the truth. She had to get on with her life...without him and without the knowledge of his feelings for her.

More than that, though, he regretted his lies. He regretted the day that Teddy would find out who he really was. Because he knew she would. Whether she discovered it on her own while going through receipts and finding the name Carlino Investigations on the top of some bill, or perhaps flipping through the Denver phone book and seeing his agency's ad, or even if Alan told her himself, Teddy *would* find out the truth.

And Mack could already feel the darkness of that day. He only hoped that when it happened, Teddy would not be too hurt by the discovery of his deceit.

He turned from her and reached for his jeans and sweater. He didn't want to leave Teddy. In fact, he wanted nothing more than to lean over and press his lips to hers and have her wake in his embrace. But he had work to do.

Padding noiselessly from the bedroom and closing the door behind him, Mack gave Bogie a cursory greeting as he headed to the kitchen. The room was chilled. Through the single bullet hole in the window's upper pane, a cold draft whistled in.

He stood by the sink and looked through the web of cracks radiating from the hole. His gaze traveled from the ax in the wood block, along the thin path he'd made through the snow yesterday morning, to the edge of the woods—the very spot where Bogie had found the fresh tracks around the tree.

Last night, during the few moments when he had slept, he'd done so lightly, listening to the night, hoping that Bogie would warn them of any danger. And more than a few times, while Teddy slept in his arms, Mack had eyed his gun on the nightstand.

The bullet made no sense. He'd tried to convince Teddy that it had been a poacher, but he put no faith in that theory. No poacher in his right mind would risk being so close to the cabin.

Taking a paring knife from one drawer, Mack turned to face the wall behind him. He located the slug buried in the drywall, and worked the knife into the neat hole. Edging the blade against the rim of the slug, he pried it back gradually, careful not to scratch the riflings that would serve as valuable evidence if his suspicions were correct.

When the lead slug dropped into his hand, Mack rolled it in his palm before clenching his fist around it. He stood and faced the window again. No, it was obvious that the bullet was meant for one of them. But who? He hadn't been lying when he'd told Teddy that he wasn't in any kind of trouble. And there certainly wasn't anyone *he* knew of that carried a grudge deep enough to go through the hassle of tracking him all the way out here on an assignment.

No. The bullet had been intended for Teddy. The thought settled on him as coldly as the air whistling through the hole in the window. In his head, Mack replayed last night: they'd been standing at the sink together, Teddy had accepted his offer for lunch, she'd smiled, he had turned and Teddy stepped away. And that was when the shot had been fired. If he hadn't moved when he did, Mack realized, gauging the angle of the bullet's path, Teddy would have been shot.

But by whom? Who knew she was up here? It had taken Mack an entire week to find her. Who else could know? Unless Alan Somerton had hired someone else...someone to trail Mack.

Why, though? And why would Somerton want Teddy shot? It was only a hunch, but the more Mack thought about it, the stronger the hunch became. And if Somerton *was* trying to kill Teddy, Mack thought, he had to get her out of Birdseye. Fast.

He started when Teddy came up behind him and wrapped her arms around his waist. He'd been so focused on the dreadful possibility of Somerton wanting to kill her that he hadn't heard the bedroom door open.

She nuzzled his ear and nestled her face into the curve of his neck. "I woke up and you weren't there. I thought you'd left," she told him, her voice still thick with sleep. "What are you doing out here?"

Mack turned. Tucking the slug into the back pocket of his jeans, he placed his hands on her hips. "I was just thinking that we should probably go into Birdseye and get a new pane of glass."

She nodded. But he could see that the window wasn't high on her list of concerns at the moment. She slid her hands past his shoulders and entwined her fingers through his hair.

She shifted enticingly closer, pinning him against the counter, and those half-lidded gray eyes were enough to make him regret having left her bed. When his gaze roved downward, from her delectable lips and to the low V of her robe where he could feel the heat rising from her, Mack pulled Teddy to him, accepting her deep kiss.

His hands traveled the length of her robed torso, caressing the curves that he knew so intimately now. And when her hips embraced his already straining erection, Mack knew that Teddy was enjoying the power she had over him.

But he couldn't give in. No more. If Teddy was in danger, he needed to maintain his perspective. And there was no way he could do that while in her enchanting embrace.

Reluctantly, he eased her back, recognizing the disappointment in her eyes, and a frustration that he himself felt all too keenly.

"Teddy, I—"

"It's all right, Mack. There's nothing to explain." She stepped away, and he watched a fleeting smile cross her lips. "You're right. It's morning. Time to move on. No regrets."

She pressed her fingertips against his lips as if to seal the secret they would carry with them from this place. "I...I'll go and get dressed."

And watching Teddy cross the cabin, knowing that he might never touch her again, Mack's knuckles whitened as his hands clenched the edge of the counter.

BOGIE WHINED SOFTLY from the back of the Jeep. Teddy wasn't surprised that the dog sensed the silent tension widening between her and Mack as they headed into Birdseye. She reached behind her and ran her fingers through the dog's thick coat when he nudged his cold nose under her ear.

Teddy glanced over to Mack, his concentration focused on the twisting mountain road, his fingers wrapped around the wheel. And as she remembered the magic those same hands had worked last night, she experienced that familiar swell of desire. With a rampant heat, it swept through her, bringing a shudder of fervent images of their lovemaking, and Teddy had to resist the urge to place her hand on Mack's thigh.

How could she simply ignore what had happened last night? How could she put something that powerful behind her?

Mack had made her feel so alive. More alive than she'd ever felt before. He'd filled her with a passion so exhilarat-

ing that it seemed as though her life was only now just beginning.

She'd never felt anything remotely close to that from
Alan, the man she'd thought she would marry and spend
the rest of her life with. But then, her entire relationship
with Alan had been conducted in much the same fashion as
any other Logan deal—formal and businesslike, practical,
and almost spiritless. And she'd truly believed that was ac-
ceptable.

For more than a year she'd been fooling herself. She'd
thought what she felt for Alan was love, but she hadn't even
seen love's full potential until last night, until she'd looked
into Mack's eyes.

And now that she'd found it, could she honestly sit back
and watch it walk away? Could she let Mack just pass
through her life?

Teddy dragged her gaze from him. She wasn't sure what
she could possibly say to change Mack's mind, but she had
to say something. And just when Teddy was about to open
her mouth, a red Jimmy careened around the corner.

MACK HAD SEEN the Jimmy seconds before it barreled into
the turn in a blaze of red. He'd noticed it through the trees,
motionless, as though sitting in the roadway idling. And
when it blasted into action, Mack was almost certain that the
driver had been waiting for them.

Gripping the wheel in both hands, Mack's only thought
was for Teddy's safety. From the corner of his eye, he saw
her brace herself, one hand gripping the edge of her seat, the
other reaching for the dash.

"Oh my God."

Mack barely heard her panicked whisper.

He lay his hand on the Jeep's horn. It was pointless. The
other driver's motive was clear—he intended to drive them

off the road. The Jimmy barreled up the narrow pass directly toward them, hugging the right bank. Snow sprayed back from beneath its tires as the driver gunned the engine. Rapidly the distance between them closed, and Mack started braking.

But reducing their speed was not bound to improve their situation by much. The Jimmy was on a destructive course, aimed directly at them, swallowing up precious road with those churning wheels. It was so close that Mack could already make out the numbers on its plates.

The only opening lay to the left, he realized as a wave of adrenaline lashed through him. To the left and down the mountainside.

Beyond the buried guardrail, there was only sky...and hundreds of feet of sheer, rugged cliff.

"Teddy, hang on. Just hang on."

And then everything spun into slow motion. Mack cranked the steering wheel to the left in that final second and gunned the engine. But it wasn't enough. The Jimmy's front bumper caught their tail end with a jarring force. Metal shrieked against metal. The Jeep whipped mercilessly to the right.

There was a blur of red and white as the Jeep lurched into its first three-sixty-degree spin. Snow and gravel ground under the wide tires. The wheel twisted uselessly in Mack's hands, skinning his bare palms.

It was on their second sickening turn that Mack was certain they were destined to sail over the guardrail and plunge to their deaths, but in that instant he felt the Jeep's tires grip. With the brake pedal to the floor, and a final wrench of the wheel, Mack brought the Jeep to a shuddering stop inches from the left bank.

"Teddy?" He closed his hand over hers, not surprised to

feel it tremble in his grasp. The blood had drained from her face. "Teddy? Are you okay?"

He waited for her wide-eyed nod and turned his gaze out the driver's-side window. The Jimmy was long gone.

When he looked at Teddy again, she was twisted in her seat, checking on Bogie. But the dog seemed to be in better shape than she was. Mack reached over and pressed his hand to her cheek.

"Are you *sure* you're all right?"

"I'm fine, Mack." She gave him a faltering smile. "I'm just glad you were driving. I don't know if I could have kept us on the road."

Mack slipped the Jeep into reverse and backed away from the bank.

"I don't want to sound paranoid, Mack," she said as he pulled the emergency brake and they got out to examine the broad dent that marred the rear of the passenger side, "but I'd have to say that either that was an extremely lousy driver, or someone is really trying to kill you."

"Come on, let's just get to Birdseye," he suggested after inspecting the underside of the Jeep. "I think you could use something to eat. And I've got some phone calls to make."

THE INCIDENT had nothing to do with bad driving. Mack had known that from the moment he'd seen the Jimmy. What he *didn't* know, however, was why? First the shooting, then a game of chicken along a dangerous mountain pass. If he was someone hired by Somerton, the man was going to great lengths to make it look like an accident. Mack realized that as soon as he'd seen the second set of tracks outside the cabin this morning.

He'd gone out while Teddy was in the shower. He'd found the new tracks, slightly snowed in, but clear nonetheless. And gauging the angle of the shot, Mack knew that the shooter had waited along the perimeter of the clearing. He'd watched Mack and Teddy, obviously waiting for Sly, Rick and Maryanne to leave, and then he'd let off one round. No more. Because one round could be written off as a stray bullet, perhaps from a poacher; but more than one would have raised suspicion.

From behind the bar of Sly's Tavern, Mack looked across the empty room to where Sly tried to comfort Teddy in one of the side booths. She didn't need much comforting though. By the time they'd parked out front, Teddy already seemed in complete control.

She was tough, Mack thought as he watched her laugh at something Sly told her.

He picked up the receiver of the bar phone, his gaze leaving Teddy only long enough to allow him to dial his office number. He'd already tried to reach Blake at headquarters, with no luck. Now, as he listened to the hollow rings, he prayed that his secretary, Ruby, was in.

She picked up on the fourth ring.

"G'mornin', Carlino Investigations."

"Hi, Ruby."

"Mack!"

He heard her chair snap back, and imagined she'd been lounging behind her desk with her feet up.

"My God, Mack, where are you? It's been crazy around here. Calls, calls, calls."

"I'm still out of town, Ruby. Sorry. Who's been trying to reach me?"

"Only everybody and their cousin's dog." He heard the rustle of papers as she collected his messages. "You've got a few calls from Mr. Kapinsky on the Levin case. And Richard Harvey wants to know if you'll do some work for him on that McBurney trial he's prosecuting. And, oh, yeah, Mr. Saulnier called five times and wants that—"

"Look, Ruby, I'll deal with all of those once I get back."

"And when's that?"

"Soon. Listen, did Detective Tennyson contact you at all?"

"Oh, yeah. He called yesterday morning. Told me to tell you he came up with squat on Somerton."

"Damn."

"That's not the same Somerton you're working for right now, is it? The same guy who's been driving me nuts with calls?"

"Somerton's been trying to reach me?"

"Yeah. He's been calling all the time. And he even came by."

"He came to the office personally?"

"Yeah."

"And what did he want?"

"To talk to you. Said he didn't require your services any longer. That he wanted to pay you what he owes you."

"Did he say *why* he didn't require my services?"

"Yeah. Something about him and his wife—"

"His fiancée."

"Whatever. He says that they're going to work things out. He said he'd heard from her and that everything's ironed out between 'em. So does this mean you're headin' home now?"

But Mack barely heard Ruby's last question. He looked across the bar and watched Teddy laugh again. She couldn't have spoken to Alan Somerton. Mack had been with her ever since he'd located her. There had never been an opportunity for her to call Denver. And even if she had, Mack was certain she would have told him about it—she'd been so honest about everything so far.

"Mack? Are you still there?"

"Yes, Ruby. I'm here. Listen, I need you to contact Detective Tennyson and get him to run a tag number." He gave her the first half of the numbers he'd managed to get off the plate of the Jimmy and told Ruby the vehicle make. After asking her to be sure Blake rushed the trace, Mack hung up.

When he looked over at Teddy again, she caught his stare briefly from the booth. The intimacy of the smile she gave him was unmistakable, and Mack wished that it didn't have the kind of power over him that it did. He needed to maintain his perspective.

Especially now. It was more than a suspicion, Mack thought. If Alan Somerton was suddenly determined to have Mack off the case, it was obvious the man had other plans. Somerton had no intention of talking to his fiancée. He wanted her dead.

Mack was almost certain of that. Whatever deranged motive he had, Alan Somerton must have hired someone...the man behind the wheel of the red Jimmy. The man with the gun.

And it was Mack's fault that Teddy's life was now in danger. It was *his* trail that had been tracked to Birdseye, not Teddy's. If it hadn't been for him, she would be safe up here.

He had to get her out of town. Away from Birdseye, away from whoever Alan had sent after them. As the first of Sly's customers shuffled in through the front door, Mack replaced the phone under the bar and went to Teddy. Sly gave him a nod as he vacated the booth.

"What's wrong, Mack?" Teddy asked him, obviously recognizing his disquiet before he'd even sat down. She reached across the table and took his hands in hers. "Who were you talking to?"

He studied their entwined fingers for a moment and when he lifted his gaze to meet hers, Mack knew he couldn't tell Teddy the truth. If he so much as whispered the possibility that her fiancé may have hired someone to kill her, he knew she would take it into her head to stay and fight. He'd seen the determination...no, the stubbornness that Teddy was capable of. Yes, she'd run away from Alan Somerton because she'd needed space, but Teddy Logan had too much damned pride to run away from danger. And it was that very defiance, the relentless determination that Mack loved in Teddy, that could get her killed. Unless he continued with the lies.

"Mack? Who did you call? Was it the sheriff?"

"No."

"Sly's determined to speak to the authorities. To report the shooting and the accident."

"That's fine. I think he should. But I can't."

"What do you mean?"

"I don't have time to stick around here." He gave her hands a gentle squeeze.

"Mack, what's going on? Please tell me."

He lowered his gaze to their hands again, unable to look her in the eye. "Teddy, I was just on the phone with a friend on the force. My ex-partner. It seems that one of our cases has come back to haunt us."

"What are you saying, Mack?"

"There's a guy we put away when we were with Narcotics. He's on parole. And word on the street is that he's out to get even."

"So someone *is* after you?"

Mack nodded.

"Then all the more reason to talk to the sheriff. They have to find this guy. They have to protect you, Mack."

"Teddy, there's nothing the local authorities can do."

"Why not? That's insane, of course there is."

"Not without proof."

"Proof? Have you forgotten that you were shot at last night? That's not proof?"

"Not enough, Teddy. The authorities would have to present more than a bullet for a judge to grant an arrest warrant. And even then, they'd have to find the guy. No, at this point there's not much anyone can do."

When he looked at her, Mack felt ashamed at her belief in him.

"So what are you going to do?" She clasped his hands even tighter now, and he hated himself all the more.

"I don't want to involve you in this, Teddy."

"I'm already involved, Mack."

"How's that?"

"Whoever is after you, they've obviously followed you up here, right?"

"Yes."

"And no doubt they've been watching the cabin for at least a couple of days. So who's to say that they won't make a move on me? Use me to get to you?"

It was working. Not only did she believe that *he* was the one in danger, but Mack felt confident that if it was *Teddy's* idea that she go with him, her stubbornness would ensure that she stayed with him. And as long as she was with him, he could protect her.

"You're right," he said. "That's why I think you should go back home. It's not safe here. And you're not safe with me."

"I'm not going home."

"But you said yourself, you can't stay here."

"That's right. That's why I'm coming with you."

"Teddy—"

"Mack, I'm not arguing about this. It's decided."

"We can't go back to the cabin. Not now. It's too risky."

"Fine. Then we leave from here. We take the Jeep." She withdrew one hand from his grasp and snatched up the car keys.

God, how he hated himself for lying to her! Especially when he looked into her eyes and saw the genuine affection and concern there. But the important thing was, Teddy was going to leave Birdseye...with him. And he could protect her.

"Are you sure about this, Teddy?" he had to ask.

"Sure?" The smile she gave him then sent a hot wave of longing directly from his heart to his groin. "Mack, I don't think I've been more sure about anything than I have this week."

"All right then. Let's go." He followed her from the booth.

"So, do you want to tell me where we're headed?" she asked as he helped her with her coat.

"Back to Denver."

He had expected the apprehension that darkened her expression when she turned to face him, and if they hadn't been standing in the middle of Sly's Tavern with customers filing in, Mack would have kissed her in an effort to ease her worry. Instead, he could only reach over and touch her slightly trembling lips with his thumb.

"I've got a friend in Denver, Teddy. Someone on the force who can help us figure this out."

She nodded, clearly still unsure.

"You won't have to go home, Teddy," he told her. "I promise."

11

THEY'D DRIVEN for hours, stopping once for gas and again for dinner at a greasy spoon when it was obvious Mack needed a break. Still, they hadn't gotten farther than ninety miles east of Craig. Sly had warned them of the impending storm when they'd said their hurried goodbyes back in Birdseye, but his weather source hadn't been entirely accurate. Nor had the radio forecaster predicted the violent winds and the sudden whiteouts that had forced Mack to slow the Jeep to a crawl for the past three hours.

Through the darkness and a wall of snow, they had seen the lights of the roadside convenience store and pulled in. Ten minutes later, Teddy had stopped pacing and leaned back against the rear panel of the Jeep, waiting for Mack as Bogie huddled by her side. Beyond the store's wide awning, freezing wind whipped the snow into violent flurries in the overhead lights. Beyond that, there was only darkness.

A short blast of wind swept in under the overhang, and Teddy felt the cold brush of snow against her face. She pulled her coat tighter around her and watched the storm. The one good thing about this blizzard, she thought, was that they had almost certainly lost whoever was after Mack. At first, they'd kept an eye on the rearview and side mirrors, but the farther they'd gotten out of Birdseye the more they realized that it was unlikely anyone could tail them through this.

Even if they were being followed, Teddy felt safe with

Mack. She didn't exactly relish the idea of returning to Denver right now, but no matter where they went, she knew she was in good hands with Mack. And in more ways than one.

Within the close confines of the Jeep, Teddy had found herself replaying last night in her mind. And as they slowly closed the distance to Denver, she wondered more and more if she could let Mack walk out of her life without at least attempting to tell him how she felt.

"Sounds like it's going to get worse before it gets better." Mack came around the hood of the Jeep, balancing a paper bag under one arm. "The kid behind the counter says that most of the secondary roads are already closed. I doubt we can get much farther in this, Teddy."

She only nodded, watching the wind ruffle his black hair as he opened the back of the Jeep and set the bag inside.

"Apparently there's a motel down the road a bit. Maybe we should call it a night," he suggested, waiting for Bogie to jump into the back before closing the Jeep.

"Teddy? What's the matter?"

If he hadn't reached out and lifted her chin with one finger, Teddy might have simply shrugged and said, "Nothing." But the physical contact reminded her of how badly she wanted to be with Mack.

"Teddy, what is it?"

She took in a deep breath of icy air. "I...I'm leaving Alan."

It didn't matter how many times she'd said the words in her head. Out loud, they sounded as if they came from someone else's lips.

"What?"

"I'm leaving Alan," she repeated, needing to hear it herself a second time. "Calling off the engagement."

She studied his reaction, not sure what to make of his silence or the unflinching stare he gave her.

She looked away, past Mack and past the awning to the

storm around them. "It's not because of you, Mack," she explained. "I mean, yes, it *is* because of you, but not...well, it's not because of *us*. It's not like I expect you to stay or anything. I know you have a life waiting for you in Boise, with your brother, and that once this is all sorted out you're leaving Denver..."

A burst of wind tugged at her hair. She lifted a hand and raked it back, angry with herself for not finding the words.

"God! I don't know anymore." Tears stung her eyes. "I don't know what I'm doing here. I don't know what I'm trying to say to you, Mack, but...I...I just thought I should tell you. That's all."

If he had taken her into his arms then, Teddy was sure she would have cried. Instead, Mack placed his hands on her shoulders and held her at arm's length.

"Teddy?" He waited until she met his gaze. "Teddy, listen to me. I don't think this is the time to talk about it. We're both under a lot of pressure right now. A lot has happened over the past couple of days. I'm not sure either of us is in any frame of mind to make decisions about the future until we've dealt with the present."

She nodded. What else was there to say? That she thought she was falling in love him? No, she couldn't admit that. Not when his life lay in an opposite direction from hers.

Mack reached up to brush the snow from her hair. When he lowered his hand again, he let one warm finger trace the line of her lips.

"Why don't we see if we can find that motel," he suggested quietly and reached for the door handle.

MACK PACED the length of the motel room for what had to be the hundredth time. He paused at the window, drew back one corner of the mustard-colored curtain and watched the whirlwind of snow that enshrouded the lights of the main office. A small convoy of storm-stranded trucks loomed in the darkness at the far end of the parking lot. He and Teddy had been lucky to get one of the last rooms. Even luckier that it wasn't a double, Mack thought as he let the curtain fall back and turned to look at the two single beds.

He wanted to keep his head about him. And sharing a bed with Teddy tonight would be begging for disaster.

He didn't believe that they would be found here—they'd paid in cash and used false names. They were more than likely safe for the time being.

He'd been down this route before. Someone's life *was* at risk. Just like his last case on the force. The only difference between then and now was that this time he was not going to screw up. He was *not* going to lose focus.

Mack paced again. Bogie watched him from where he lay between the two beds. The dog's head rested on his forepaws, his lazy gaze following Mack's path.

"What are you looking at?" Mack asked. "And don't tell me you've never felt this way about some primped-up poodle that's caught your eye."

Bogie whined softly, and continued watching him.

Mack stopped in the middle of the room, buried his hands in the pockets of his jeans and watched steam tumble out through the partially open door of the bathroom. He listened to the sound of water striking the sides of the shower stall. It didn't take much imagination to picture Teddy in that shower, hot water sluicing down the supple curves of her naked body. Or to imagine his hands on that wet and willing flesh, touching all those places he'd explored last night, places that he knew so intimately.

No! He had to maintain his distance. Keep his mind on the case. He wished he could call Blake and get the information on the tag number from the Jimmy. But even if Blake had the information already, it wouldn't do him any good right now, stuck in this motel room.

Mack rolled his shoulders, trying to ease the tension that had been building there since this morning. The hours of driving through whiteouts and drifting snow hadn't helped. Neither had hours of sitting only inches from Teddy in the tight confines of the Jeep.

From the moment they'd left Birdseye, her hand had rested on his thigh, her palm hot through the denim of his jeans. He'd welcomed the physical contact, needing it as much as Teddy seemed to. Even when she'd dozed off for a half hour just outside of Craig, her hand hadn't left his leg. He shouldn't have been surprised at how that minor contact had been enough to cause his mind to wander, toying with memory and fantasy, threatening to distract him from his driving. It didn't take much with Teddy. Just like now.

Water drummed against the porcelain tub. Mack closed his eyes and let out a long sigh as he felt the familiar tug in his gut.

She was leaving Alan. Mack could still picture the way her eyes had glistened when she'd told him at the truck stop. He'd seen she was close to tears, even though he hadn't known why exactly—whether she was upset or still unsure of her decision, or if it was the fact that she believed Mack was heading off to Boise. God, how he'd wanted to take her into his arms and hold her. Hold her tightly, and tell her how much it pained him to look at her because he couldn't be with her.

And it was that same sweet pain that drew Mack to the open bathroom door now. He knew he shouldn't. Knew what would happen as soon as he saw her. And he knew there would be no controlling the longing that raged through his entire body as he imagined her in that shower. But it was killing him to know she was that close.

He forced back the voice in his head—the voice that told him he had to protect Teddy, that he couldn't let his emotions get in the way of his duty—and he reached for the edge of the door. He eased it open the rest of the way, a cloud of steam greeting him. Behind the frosted glass of the shower enclosure, he saw the blurred outline of Teddy's figure, but his memory easily filled in the details, defining every angle and curve with vivid clarity.

She stood under the steady stream, unmoving, her head tilted back as she let the water run over her.

"Teddy?"

She didn't start when he whispered her name. It was as though she had been expecting it. Expecting him. Wanting him as much as he wanted her now.

She said nothing when she slid open the glass door. And as Mack took in the vision of her standing there, naked and wet before him, even more beautiful than he remembered, he knew there was no turning back. She reached across the narrow bathroom, snatching the edge of his shirt between her fingers, and drew him toward her. Silently, she undid each button and tugged the ends from his waistband.

Her eyes never left his. Even when she brushed back his shirt, dropping it to the floor, and trailed her wet fingers down his torso, her silvery gaze held his. He saw the slight smile on her lips—seductive, anxious, knowing.

She unbuttoned his jeans, and worked the fly down over his already straining erection. And when she slid her hand, hot and wet, beneath the thin fabric of his boxers and took hold of him, Mack's breath hitched.

"Are you coming in? Or do I have to come out there and get you?" she murmured, stroking him slowly.

Mack slid his jeans and shorts over his hips, discarding them along with his shirt, and in seconds he closed the stall door behind him. Steam billowed through the small enclosure, swirling around them, drawing their bodies together. Water streamed over his shoulders and back, easing the tension there. But now a new tension gripped him as he took Teddy into his arms.

When he kissed her this time, he was struck by her assuredness. There wasn't a hint of hesitancy in the way her mouth claimed his. Her lips parted his, her fingers fanned through his wet hair, and she pulled him ever deeper into the intoxicating passion of her kiss.

The day's events were lost to him. Nothing mattered except his driving need to be with Teddy. Gone was reason, the voice in his head that had whispered danger, that had tried to remind him of his past, the voice that told him they had no future.

Hot water flowed over both of them, washing away everything except the keen hunger. Teddy pressed her body even tighter against his, pinning his erection against her soft belly, an agonizing reminder of how much he wanted to be inside her. Mack slid his hands up her back, along her rib cage, and cupped one breast in each palm. He lowered his lips to the already erect nipples, sucking each hard, round bud until he heard Teddy's throaty moan.

Bringing his mouth back up to hers, he licked the water from her lips. And when her hands glided over his shoulders and across his chest, Mack felt the smile that curved her lips under his. Seconds later he realized what that smile was for.

With his back to the wall of the shower stall, Mack was under Teddy's power. As she trailed her fingers down his torso, her mouth followed. Her relentless kisses burned along his skin, even hotter than the water from the shower, moving steadily downward. Her fingertips shivered across his groin and along the inside of his thighs. And as she took his hard shaft into both hands and started her slow, skillful stroking, Mack felt the delicious shocks of longing lick through him.

But that was nothing compared to Teddy's mouth. Teddy's sweet, clever, tantalizing mouth.

She ran the tip of her tongue along his full length, and even before he felt her lips close around his aroused flesh, Mack thought he was going to shatter. Her mouth was exquisite, her seduction sublime. He could no longer suppress the moan that seemed to rip from the very center of his being as he reached down and wove his fingers through Teddy's wet hair.

When finally she allowed him to draw her mouth up to his again and Mack felt the length of her body press longingly against his, he wasn't certain he'd ever come as close to the brink of passion as Teddy had taken him, without falling into its fiery abyss.

And still that mouth worked wonders. In her kiss, Mack could feel Teddy's own yearning as distinctly as his own, rising beyond anything they'd yet experienced. An urgent hunger that belonged to two people who might never again share the kind of passion they were sharing tonight.

"Oh, Teddy...I...I don't think I can hold out any longer."

"Then don't." Her whisper was ragged against his ear.

"I want to be inside you."

Her hands slid past his waist, taking hold of him and guiding him to her.

"Teddy—"

"I want you, Mack."

He held her face in his hands, staring into gray eyes, seeing the longing there, seeing the love.

"I want you," she whispered again.

And then Mack entered her, feeling her liquid heat envelop him, drawing him in where he knew she wanted him. Nothing between them now, only hot willing flesh against flesh. He wanted to savor that sensation, to enter her slowly and make it last all night, but he couldn't. He wanted Teddy now. Wanted her completely. Body and soul.

He took her in his arms, his hands on her buttocks, and lifted her from the floor of the shower. Her long legs circled his waist as he turned her so that 'her back was braced against the wall this time. She wrapped her arms around his neck, clinging to him as he kissed her mouth with almost savage desire. And as he thrust deeper and deeper into that delicious ecstasy that was Teddy, as he brought her down onto his length, he heard her moan.

She threw her head back, crying his name. His arms trembled as he held her and he could feel the tremors of her climax ripple through her, clenching him even tighter inside her. She was on the very brink of that rapture, and he was dying to go there with her.

"Teddy."

"Please, Mack," she pleaded for him now, wanting his release as keenly as he did. "Don't hold back. I want you, Mack. I love you."

With those last three words Mack plunged into her one final time, losing himself completely to the driving white-hot pulse that lashed through him. And as he clasped Teddy in his arms, her wet body still convulsing with a deep pleasure matched only by his own, Mack climaxed with her, filling her in fierce and feverish bursts until he had nothing left to give.

THE AIR BRAKES of a semitransport in the parking lot let out a second long-winded squeal, but Teddy had woken at the sound of the first one. The room was still cloaked in darkness. There was no daylight behind the window by the door, only the sickly green glow of the motel lights through the heavy yellow curtains.

She didn't move, but remained wedged in the firm angles of Mack's body. With her head nestled between his shoulder and chest, she felt the steady rise and fall of his breathing and listened to the low rhythm of his heart.

At first Mack had offered to push the two single beds together, but after Mack had wrapped her in a thick towel and carried her to one of the beds, there had been no need to. He'd pulled back the covers, lowered Teddy to the sheets and then joined her. Their skin had still been damp, their bodies still hot from the passion they had shared.

Mack had held her close on the narrow bed, spooning her against his powerful body. He'd caressed her with his broad hands, threatening to take her to that brink once more, and Teddy had felt his growing arousal again, hot and hard against the small of her back. But Mack seemed to quell his own desire, and soon his touches became more comforting than arousing. And when he'd spoken at last, there was deep concern in his voice.

"Teddy," he'd whispered, brushing her damp hair with his fingers. "We didn't use anything."

"I know."

"Are you sorry it happened?"

She'd turned in his arms so that she could look into his handsome face, and laid a hand on his cheek. "Sorry? No." She shook her head, remembering how alive she'd felt with him inside her. "No, Mack, I wanted you. I wanted to be with you."

"But it was a mistake, Teddy."

"Was it?"

"You don't think it was?"

She'd searched his gaze, not certain what she'd hoped to find there, and finally she'd turned again, nestling against him, needing to feel his embrace. His arms tightened around her. He rested his chin on her shoulder, and when he nuzzled her ear, he pressed a tender kiss to her neck.

"Teddy? You don't think it was a mistake?"

"I don't know, Mack," she answered him at last. "I don't know what to think anymore, to tell you the truth."

She'd reached up then, grasping his hands in hers and drew his arms even tighter around her, never wanting to leave the shelter of his embrace. "Hold me, Mack," she'd whispered to him. "Just hold me."

And he did. In the silence of the room, as the last of the storm's severity played itself out beyond the walls of the motel, Mack held her. Minutes grew into hours, and neither broke the intimacy of their embrace.

It was only much later that Teddy heard Mack speak again. But this time she detected a waver in his whisper—so quiet that she was certain Mack believed her to be asleep.

"I love you, Teddy," he'd murmured into the dark silence, and the anguish in his voice filled her with sweet sorrow.

She'd lain awake in his arms long after that, long after she was certain he'd found sleep, and she thought about his admission. If she'd had any doubts about what they'd done in the shower, those were banished now. And if Mack truly did love her, then maybe it *wasn't* insane to dream of a future with him.

As Teddy eased herself from Mack's embrace, and slipped out from under the covers, she studied his strong features, calm in sleep. She wanted to touch him, to kiss those firm lips, but resisted. She wouldn't wake him—she'd seen the exhaustion in his face after the strenuous drive. From the nightstand, she checked Mack's watch, tilting it to catch the sallow light from the motel sign—five a.m.

Teddy searched the dark floor and located her jeans. She needed something to drink. The dry heat of the room had made her incredibly thirsty, and she was already imagining the rewards of the cold but short trip she'd make to the lobby's vending machine.

From the other bed, Bogie lifted his head and yawned as he watched her reach for the sweater from the vinyl chair. Mack's sweater. Teddy pulled it over her head and smelled the lingering trace of his after-shave. She breathed deeply, the familiarity of his scent sending warm contentment swelling through her as she glanced toward his sleeping form once more.

Bogie joined her at the door, stretching his limbs and whining softly. She shushed him and looked around quickly for her coat. When she spotted it on the far side of the room, Teddy took Mack's instead and shrugged the ample leather jacket over her shoulders before slipping out into the cold night.

The storm had relented. Delicate crystalline snowflakes danced in the pale shafts of light from the parking-lot lamps. Out on the road, a plow thundered by, its flashing blue lights strobing through the morning darkness. At the other end of the lot, some of the trucks had already left, resuming their scheduled routes.

Teddy cut her own trail across the parking lot to the main office while Bogie wandered through the belly-deep snow. When she reached the front of the motel, she squinted against the bright glare of the lobby lights through the glass entrance. She was already fingering the change in her jeans' pockets and eyeing the pop machine in the entranceway as she pulled open the door.

The woman behind the front counter lifted her head from the cradle of her arms and gave Teddy a bleary-eyed gaze. Teddy waved and turned to the vending machine. As she counted out quarters and dimes, she was again struck by the seductive scent lifting from Mack's sweater and mingling with the smell of worn leather. She couldn't resist a smile as she thought about what they'd done in the shower last night.

From the moment she'd stepped into the shower, she had hoped Mack would join her. That's why she'd left the bathroom door partly ajar. When she'd heard his voice whisper her name, she was almost instantly wet...and not from the shower. She'd wanted to be with him so badly that when she'd opened the stall door and seen him standing there before her, Teddy had felt her knees weaken. And when she'd unzipped his jeans and slipped her hand inside, feeling how ready Mack was for her, she'd thought she would explode right then.

It had been different than the night before. In the shower, there had been a far greater urgency to their lovemaking, a driving hunger that had overridden every last vestige of restraint. And then, when she'd guided Mack into her, drawing him so deep inside, there had been nothing more heavenly than the feel of her flesh surrounding his.

With the water crashing over them, Mack's power had consumed her. His mouth had crushed hers, and his thrusts had driven her back against the shower wall as his fingers dug into the soft flesh of her buttocks. It had been a savage ecstasy.

"D'you need change?"

Teddy felt a flush race to her cheeks, wondering how long she'd been standing there in the lobby, reliving last night's passion. "Pardon me?"

"For the machine," the woman behind the counter asked. "You need change?"

"Oh, no, thanks. I've got it." She gave the woman a nervous smile and turned her attention to the coins in her hand. But the truth was, she *was* short a quarter.

She checked her jeans again, then decided to look for

coins in the pockets of Mack's leather jacket. As she searched, her fingertips brushed across the smooth surface of a photograph tucked into the right-hand pocket. Teddy thought twice about pulling out the three-by-five. What right did she have to snoop through Mack's things?

Then again, after last night, what possible secrets could Mack have from her?

Teddy drew out the dog-eared photograph. The handwritten date on the back appeared oddly familiar, but it wasn't until she turned the photo over that the motel lobby began to reel around her.

Suddenly the lights overhead seemed infinitely harsher. She blinked several times, not quite believing that what she saw in her hands was real.

But it was. Dreadfully real.

She remembered the day Alan had shot the photograph. She'd just taken second prize in the hunters' class riding Chelsea's Honor. It had been several months ago. That weekend late in August. Happier days.

But only Alan had a copy of the photograph. It sat in a frame on the corner of his desk. Or at least, it *had*.

For a long time, Teddy couldn't move. She couldn't take her eyes off the picture that shook between her trembling fingers. And when finally she looked up, glancing past her own reflection in the reinforced glass, beyond the parking lot and to the dark window of their room, she knew there was only one way Mack could have gotten the photo.

And there was only one reason for him to have it.

12

WHEN MACK jolted awake, it took him a few hazy seconds to recognize the motel room. His nerves eased from the initial shock, but only for a second before he sat upright in the narrow bed.

"Teddy?"

The other bed was still made. The bathroom was dark.

"Teddy?"

Mack was already halfway across the room, calling her name a third time, when he realized that Bogie was gone, as well. Perhaps she'd taken him for a walk. Her boots and coat were gone. *Yes*, he convinced himself. *She'd taken Bogie out.*

It was daylight already. Sunshine slipped in through the thin crack between the curtains. Maybe Teddy was scouting for breakfast.

Mack reached for his jeans. He'd go and find her. He didn't like the idea of her being on her own. Sure, there was little chance they'd been followed here, but still, it wasn't safe. Not until he figured out what Alan Somerton was up to.

He'd call Blake this morning and find out if he'd uncovered anything about the driver of the Jimmy.

Once they got him, it would be only a matter of minutes before Blake had the guy turning state's evidence. Blake was one of Denver's finest in the interrogation room. Blake would be able to convince the man—no doubt Somerton's hired thug—that nothing was worth the charges he'd be up against for the target shooting he'd done the other night.

No, once they had the driver of the Jimmy, they'd have Alan Somerton. He was certain of that.

Mack tucked his shirt into the waistband of his jeans. He'd be glad to get to Denver. At least there he could actually *do* something to get to the bottom of this.

In the meantime, he had to keep Teddy safe. And he had to keep her away from the truth.

But when Mack turned to the nightstand for his watch, he froze.

He was too late.

He stared wide-eyed at the nightstand. Next to his watch, propped against the porcelain lamp base, was Teddy's picture. The photograph Somerton had given him. The photograph he'd carried for the week before he found Teddy. The photograph he'd stupidly left in his coat pocket.

And Teddy had found it.

"Damn," he cursed under his breath.

Teddy knew the truth.

"Damn. Damn...damn!" This could *not* be happening!

Mack staggered through the room, rushing to the door. But even as he reached for the handle, he knew she was gone. There was no trace of her in the room. Still...he didn't want to believe it.

Only when he threw open the door to a blast of freezing air did the cold reality hammer home. As Mack blinked against the piercing glare of the morning sun reflecting off of pristine snow, he looked to the empty space where the Jeep had been parked.

SHE'D BEEN DRIVING for three hours. Her wrists ached from gripping on the Jeep's steering wheel, although the driving conditions weren't all that bad. The plows had been through and most of the roads reopened. But Teddy's white-knuckled clench hadn't eased around the wheel since she'd backed out of the motel lot three hours ago.

After finding the photograph, she'd wandered back across the cold parking lot in a half-stupor, still wanting to believe there was a reasonable explanation behind what she'd discovered.

Even when she'd crept into their room and quietly gathered her things, Teddy had almost wanted Mack to wake up, wanted him to take her in his arms and convince her he hadn't been hired by Alan to find her—that everything they'd shared hadn't been some kind of cruel game.

But she knew better.

Bogie let out a soft whine. From where he sat in the passenger seat, he swung her another doleful gaze as though questioning why Mack was no longer with them, and whined again.

Teddy shot him an angry look. "I don't want to hear it, Bogie. You should never have let him in the cabin in the first place, you big mutt. Some judge of character you turned out to be."

The dog yawned and looked out the windshield. The Interstate 25 was only just beginning to become congested with weekend traffic. Earlier it had seemed as if she was the only driver on the road, alone in a world of white, alone with her thoughts.

But it didn't matter how many times she turned things over in her mind. Teddy didn't understand any of it. The only thing she was certain of was that Alan had hired Mack to find her.

She'd berated herself almost nonstop for not having heeded the warnings. Because the signs had been there. The night she'd driven the Jeep off the road, she'd already suspected that the tailing car might have had something to do with Alan. Then, the next morning when she'd woken to find Mack in her room, after he'd admitted to following her, a cold frisson of suspicion had shivered through her.

She should have heeded it. She should have listened to her gut.

And there had been more obvious signs after that. He'd known of Sly's cabin. He'd known her name. In fact, Mack had known entirely too much about her.

Yet, she'd been so willing to believe his explanations. Hell, she'd even racked up some of his "insights" to his experience as a cop, actually giving him credit for his intuitiveness.

God, she'd been a fool!

And a cop, of all things! On leave. Why hadn't she considered the possibility that he could be a private investigator?

But what had Alan hired Mack to do? That was the most nagging question of all. If Alan had sent him to find her, why hadn't Mack simply reported her location and left? Why hadn't she found Alan banging on the door the very next morning?

It didn't make sense. Unless Alan had hired Mack for other reasons. Reasons that Teddy couldn't even hazard a guess at. Back at the cabin, that first afternoon, she'd wondered if Mack had been poking through her papers on the desk. But what could Alan possibly think she had? And what could be worth the expense of hiring a private investigator?

It all came back to that afternoon in Alan's office. She was sure of it.

Lifting one hand from the wheel, Teddy massaged her temple. The headache had flared the moment she'd pulled that photograph out of Mack's pocket. Still now the images flashed through her mind: Mack in Alan's office at Logan Publishing, Alan handing him the photograph, and explaining what he wanted done. The very thought of Alan and Mack standing together in the same room, speaking to one another, talking about *her*...

Teddy gripped the wheel again and pressed her foot a little harder on the gas, pushing the Jeep steadily north. God, she felt so betrayed. They'd made a complete fool out of her—*both* of them. But especially Mack.

What made her anger worse was that she had only herself to blame.

She was the one who had asked Mack to make love to her. What had possessed her? And not just once...but again and again.

Never in her life had she been so foolish.

But the joke was on Mack now, she thought, placing her right hand on Bogie's neck and burying her fingers in the thick fur. She'd had the last laugh—leaving Mack stranded in a roadside motel halfway between Craig and Denver. Chances were, it would take him the better part of the day just to get to the city.

As Teddy maneuvered the Jeep to pass a slow-moving transport, she thought about Mack in that motel room. A small part of her worried about him. Worried about the fact that his life was in danger, because *that* was the one part of this whole affair that Teddy actually believed. After all, the bullet that had come through the window the other night had been real. And the driver of the Jimmy hadn't been playing games.

When Mack had set out to find Teddy, he'd probably never dreamed someone would come after *him*. And more than likely he hadn't counted on being deserted at a motel in the middle of Nowhere, Colorado.

But he'd be safe, Teddy tried to convince herself. He had his gun, and he had some cash. He'd manage to get to Denver and to his "friend" as he'd suggested he would. Mack would be safe.

Teddy laughed. She must be insane! Why in God's name was she even worrying about him! After all the lies and all the deceit, after he'd let her believe that he loved her...

No, she would push Mack Carlino out of her mind now. And forever.

As Teddy entered the Fort Collins city limits, she shoved her sunglasses farther up the bridge of her nose and resolved to put everything behind her. She'd spend the weekend with her friend Holly, and then, only then, would she return to Denver—on *her* terms—and settle things with Alan once and for all.

IT HAD TAKEN Mack seven hours to get to Denver, even though it should have been a two-and-a-half-hour drive.

First there were phone calls to make. It had been too early to reach Blake, so he'd left a message, explaining what he could and asking his ex-partner to meet him at his office.

Then Mack had called Sly, admitting everything to the bar owner: who he was, how he'd been hired to find Teddy and that she was in danger. He could only hope that Sly would contact him as promised if Teddy showed up in Birdseye. But Mack doubted that Teddy would return to the cabin immediately.

After the phone calls, Mack had scouted around for a ride. He'd caught a lift with one of the truckers staying at the motel, but by the time he and Hank hit the road, Highway 40 had been clogged with previously storm-bound traffic—all headed to Denver.

It was close to four by the time he'd said goodbye to Hank in Wheat Ridge and rented a car. And now, as Mack took the stairs to his office two at a time, he checked his watch. It was almost five.

He'd been on the lookout when he'd driven into the garage moments ago, half expecting to find the red Jimmy waiting for him.

If he'd been the link to Teddy in Birdseye, it wasn't absurd to suspect that whoever Somerton had hired might be checking out Mack's home or office, expecting them to return to Denver.

The office was empty.

But the fact that someone *wasn't* watching his office concerned Mack even more. If *he* wasn't being tracked, then someone was watching Teddy. He had to find her...before Alan Somerton did.

Mack didn't bother turning on the lights as he crossed the room to his office. Late-afternoon sunshine filtered through the oak blinds behind his desk, and in the dim shafts of pale orange Mack pulled out the Denver directory. He scanned the column of L's and reached for the phone.

As he listened to the hollow rings, Mack realized that he wasn't sure what he'd say if Teddy actually picked up on the other end of the line. He breathed a sigh of relief when an older woman answered.

"Logan residence."

"Yes, could I speak with Teddy Logan, please?"

"I'm sorry, sir, Ms. Logan is out of town."

"Do you know when she'll be back?"

"I'm sorry, no, I don't. Who shall I say called?"

"Nobody. Nobody called. Thank you," Mack answered, returning the receiver to its cradle.

So Teddy hadn't gone home. Not that he'd truly thought she would. Still, he'd had to check.

The red light on the answering machine blinked from the corner of his desk. He pressed the messages button and listened to the calls as he rummaged through his files to find the one he needed. The messages were varied, mostly from clients, one from his mother admonishing him for not having returned her calls, and another from Blake telling him he'd try again later when he had a positive ID on the license plate.

When Mack at last found his file on Teddy, he sank back in his chair and searched for the list Somerton had given him almost two weeks ago—names of Teddy's friends.

Mack scanned the list, until he found one familiar name: Holly Ryan in Fort Collins. He'd seen it when he'd rooted through Teddy's papers at the cabin. That had to be it. Teddy must have spoken to her from the road weeks ago, before she'd gone to Birdseye. That's why her address had been scrawled on the back of some take-out menu.

Mack's hand lingered on the receiver. The number was there. All he had to do was call. But what would he say? If Teddy *was* there, what could he possibly tell her over the phone?

He'd hurt her. Just as he'd known he would. Only, it had happened a lot sooner than he'd counted on.

How many times in the past eight hours had he envisioned Teddy's shock at finding the photo in his jacket pocket? Imagined the betrayal and the anger she must have felt when she'd set that photo on the nightstand, only two feet away from where he lay, so that he would find it in the morning? Had she stood over him, watching him sleep, hating him for everything he'd done to her?

Mack removed his hand from the receiver. No. He couldn't do this with a phone call. If Teddy *was* in Fort Collins, as his hunch told him, he had to go to her and speak with her face-to-face.

When Mack heard the faint squeak of the outer office door, instinct kicked in. He reached for his side-holster and drew out his semiautomatic. He didn't move, except to release the gun's safety, and raise it slowly. He listened to the footsteps, slow and sure, cross the front office toward his partially open door. His hand tensed around the gun's grip, steadying it.

And then he heard the jangle of loose change. Their code. It had come in handy a number of times when they'd worked undercover, and had probably saved both of their lives more than once.

"Come on in, Blake." Mack lowered the weapon.

Blake Tennyson pushed open the office door. He practically filled the doorway with his six-foot-two frame. But it was the patch over his left eye that was Blake's signature, making him look even more indomitable. Mack remembered how Blake had tried to ease the tension after the shooting two years ago, by joking that the patch would be a turn-on for women. But that point had yet to be proven. Blake was still single.

"Bit jumpy, aren't we, Mack?" Blake nodded to Mack's semiautomatic. "Were you expecting company?"

"I wasn't expecting anyone. Did you get my message?" Mack returned his gun to its holster.

"That's why I'm here."

Blake eased his body into the chair across from Mack and stretched his legs. He took a moment, looking around the office as though searching for something. When he pretended to peer under the desk, Mack finally gave in to his ex-partner's antics.

"Okay, what? What are you looking for, Blake?"

"The damsel in distress." He gave Mack a smug grin. "In your message you said something about someone using you for target practice and then trying to run the two of you off the road. I'd assumed she'd be with you."

"Well, she's not."

"So where is she?"

"I don't know. I lost her."

"You lost her? Mack, you lose a file, you lose your keys,

you lose that phantom sock in the dryer, but you don't just lose a person. You slept with her, didn't you?"

"Blake—"

"You slept with her and she took off. And now you have *no* idea where she is because *you* lost perspective."

"I know where she is, Blake."

"Oh yeah? Where?"

"Fort Collins."

"Then how come you don't sound so sure?"

"I'm sure, okay? Dammit, Blake, would you cut me some slack here? This is different than two years ago."

"How?"

"Because I love her, okay, Blake? Now...are you going to help me with this or not?"

There was a slight tilt to Blake's head then as he studied Mack with his one good eye.

"Wow," he said finally, and shook his head.

"What, 'wow'?"

"Just...I don't know. Wow. All the years I've known you, Mack, and I've never seen you like this before—so on edge. This must be serious."

"Yeah, you could say that." But "serious" didn't even begin to describe the panic that twisted in his gut when he thought of Teddy out there on her own...running into the man Alan Somerton had hired to kill her.

"So, do you have anything for me on that tag number?"

Blake nodded. "Sheldon Wagner."

Mack shrugged. "The name means nothing to me."

"Well, he's the owner of a brand-spanking-new red Jimmy."

"Do you have anything on him?"

"You mean, besides trying to run you off the road?"

Mack nodded.

"Yeah, he's got priors. Mostly small stuff. Burglary, car

theft. He just finished serving some time for armed robbery. We've used him a couple of times in the past as a snitch."

"So you actually know this guy?"

"Well enough."

"Do you think he's got the connections to take a contract for a hit?"

"I don't know, Mack. What's up? Are you thinking that Wagner's been hired to take you out?"

"Not me. Teddy. I'm probably just a bonus for the guy."

"So what have you got so far?"

Mack stood up, retrieved the slug from his pocket and dropped it into Blake's palm. "I took that out of the cabin wall in Birdseye. I'm sure once you find this Wagner character you'll find the rifle that fired it. And once I get Teddy back here, you can take some paint scrapings off the side of her Jeep. I doubt you'll have a problem matching them with Wagner's new Jimmy."

"Who's behind Wagner then? Does Teddy have any idea?"

Mack shook his head. "Right now, Teddy thinks that someone's after me, not her. I haven't exactly had a chance to tell her the truth. But I know it's Alan Somerton. I told you before, Blake, I knew he was wrong the minute I met him."

"Well, then," Blake said, standing, "I guess I'll have to see about picking up our boy Wagner and find out what he knows about this." He turned the slug over in his hand. "In the meantime, you'd better locate Teddy and put your heads together."

But even as Mack scrawled the Fort Collins address on a slip of paper and shoved it into his pocket, he doubted that he'd have much success in getting Teddy even to talk to him.

Still, he had to try. Not only because he loved her, but because her life depended on it.

13

TEDDY CLOSED her fingers around the warm mug of tea, and looked over the back of the sofa to the darkness beyond Holly's living-room window. At the other end of the small yard, in the pale yellow glow of an outdoor lamp, a light snowfall swirled to the cold ground. She set down her cup and wrapped her arms tighter around herself, drawing her knees to her chest.

From the kitchen, she could hear Holly talking softly on the phone. When it rang five minutes ago, Teddy had instantly worried that it could be Mack calling. It wasn't until Holly had answered it, that Teddy realized how ridiculous the thought had been. How could he have traced her to Fort Collins?

And why should she think of Mack anyway?

Then again, she *was* still wearing his sweater—still feeling the warm prickle of its wool collar against her skin and smelling the familiarity of his scent...

She should have asked Holly for a change of clothes.

Once she'd found Holly's new address this morning and pulled into the driveway, Teddy had been too tired to tell her friend what had happened. Instead, she'd taken a shower and crawled into the bed in the guest room Holly had made up for her. It wasn't until early this afternoon that Teddy had told her friend everything.

Everything...except what had taken place last night in the motel room. As understanding as Holly was, and as long as they'd been friends, Teddy could not bring herself to talk about last night's events until she herself could come to terms with them. If that was ever possible.

She and Mack hadn't used any protection. She'd thought it was all right. She'd thought it didn't matter because they loved each other. God, what kind of romantic foolishness had possessed her?

Had she honestly thought it would be all right if she got pregnant by Mack, that it wouldn't matter because she loved him?

No, she hadn't been thinking at all. She'd been out of her mind. Out of her mind in love...or so she'd thought.

She'd lost all ability to reason last night. But then, in all honesty, she'd lost that the minute she'd laid eyes on Mack Carlino at the bar, the second she'd woken up to find him standing next to her bed at the cabin.

Well, things were different now. She was going back to Denver tomorrow, back to work, back to her old life. She wouldn't see Mack again, she told herself.

And if she *was* pregnant? What then? Teddy closed her eyes. She couldn't think about that. Not right now. All she could do was hope.

"Teddy?"

When she opened her eyes again, Holly crossed the living room to sit on the end of the sofa.

"Do you think you should call your father at least?" Holly drew her legs up onto the couch, as well, and Teddy was suddenly reminded of all the late-night chats and sleep-overs they'd had when they were girls, when life hadn't been so damned complicated.

"No," Teddy answered. "I'll talk to my father when I go back."

Holly only nodded, neither agreeing or disagreeing. But

that was Holly—rarely asserting her opinion unless she was absolutely certain someone was making a grave error.

Teddy looked down at Bogie, and lowered a hand to his head. "You know something really weird, Holly?" she said eventually. "All these years I've been moaning about wanting to go back to Yale to finish up, and I've complained about my father's obsession with Logan Publishing...and yet, after this month away from it all, I think I've realized that I actually *do* enjoy the company. I mean, I can honestly say that I miss my work. And I know this might sound strange, but I'm looking forward to getting back."

"Don't you mean that you're looking forward to getting back so you can bury yourself in your work the same way your father does? So you don't have to face the reality around you?"

Teddy held Holly's perceptive stare.

"I know you too well, Teddy."

"All right, fine, I confess, I'm looking forward to burying myself in my work. But is that so wrong if I like the work I'm doing?"

"Even with Alan there? You know it's not going to be easy."

Teddy shook her head. "No. I realize that. But it's over between us. That's probably the one thing I know with absolute certainty right now. So if he wants to stay with the company, then...we'll simply have to learn to work around each other."

"And there's no chance that you and he—"

"None. It's over, Holly. For good."

Holly said nothing for a long time after that. They shared the comfortable silence of old friends and drank their tea. Teddy was grateful Holly recognized that the subject of Alan and their engagement was closed.

She shouldn't have been surprised however when Holly

brought up the one subject she'd been trying to forget. "So what about Mack then?"

"What about him?"

"Aren't you at least going to call him and find out if he's all right?"

"I'm sure he's fine." Teddy turned to the window again. The reflection she saw of herself there was strained with emotional exhaustion, and she wondered if she'd ever again feel the happiness she had felt in Mack's arms. It would have been easier—far easier—if he had been who he'd claimed to be, if he'd loved her for that short time and then driven to Boise and out of her life forever. At least that way she could have hung on to the memories of their time together.

Now she didn't even have those. They'd been spoiled. Stripped from her the moment she'd learned the truth. And where those memories might have warmed her, there was only cold emptiness.

"No, Holly, I'm not going to call him. That's over, as well."

"Are you sure?"

"I have to be."

"I don't think you believe that."

"Well, I've got to believe it, Holly. I have to get on with my life."

"You're telling me you don't love him?"

"How can I? Everything was a lie."

"You can't know that for certain, Teddy."

"Maybe not. But what does it matter if I love him? I'll get over it. I got over Alan." Even as Teddy heard the words leave her lips, she knew that it wasn't a relevant argument. She'd never loved Alan the way she loved...no, the way she *thought* she'd loved Mack. So comparing the two proved nothing.

"And what if he loves you? What then?"

"Then *he'll* have to get over it, won't he?" She was surprised by the bitterness she heard in her own voice.

"Look, Teddy, you know I don't butt in very often, but...I really have to say something here, because if I don't, I'll never be able to forgive myself."

"Holly—"

"No, Teddy. You don't have to listen to my advice, but I have to get it off my chest."

Teddy looked down to where her fingers were buried in Bogie's thick coat. She couldn't meet the intensity of Holly's stare. Considering how seldom Holly offered advice, and knowing that it had almost always been the best she ever received, Teddy wondered if she was ready to hear what her friend had to say.

"Teddy, listen to me. Love...true love, that is, doesn't come around every day, let alone every lifetime. From what you've told me, and from what I can see in your eyes, this *is* one of those. You know it, Teddy, don't you? And if I'm right, if your *heart* is right, then you *can't* just walk away from him."

God, she wanted to believe that. More than anything, Teddy wanted to believe the whole thing hadn't been a lie, that Mack hadn't stayed with her to fulfill some covert plan of Alan's. She wanted to believe they had shared true love.

"Why can't you at least talk to him, Teddy? At least give him a chance to tell his side of the story."

Teddy let out a long breath. It hurt so much, the ache inside, the part of her that wished she was still back at the cabin...with Mack, before she'd learned the awful truth, before reality had shattered the love she thought she'd found.

"One phone call, Teddy. The way I see it, you've got nothing to lose...and absolutely everything in the world to gain."

MACK PARKED the rental car alongside the curb of Paseo Drive and took the keys from the ignition. Wiping the haze from the driver's-side window with the back of his glove, he looked across the street to the squat split-level bungalow. The porch light illuminated the brass 15.

But he hadn't needed to see the house number to know he'd found the right address. From halfway down the block he'd spotted the black Jeep Wrangler glistening under the street lamp at the end of the driveway. The sight of it had sent relief rippling through every muscle.

Now, that relief tightened to tension as he thought about seeing Teddy again. What would he say to her? What *could* he say to make up for all those lies?

During the hour drive from Denver to Fort Collins, Mack had rehearsed the words he hoped might convince Teddy of his feelings for her. Yet each time he stumbled through the various speeches in his head, they all sounded empty.

No, there was nothing he could tell Teddy to persuade her that he loved her. So, for now, he'd have to put love aside. The most important thing was that he convince her of the danger she was in. *If* she would even talk to him.

He prayed she would. Her life would depend on her faith in him. Even though Mack doubted that Teddy had a lot of faith left after what he'd done to her.

But he *would* protect her. No matter what.

What Mack needed now was something concrete on Alan Somerton, something he could give to Blake so they could move on the guy. It wasn't enough to sit back and hope that Blake and his men would find Sheldon Wagner, let alone wring the truth out of the hardened ex-con.

Besides which, Wagner could have easily ditched the rifle he'd used to take that shot at them. He could have unloaded the Jimmy, traded it in, given it to a friend, whatever. And then they'd have nothing—no ballistics evidence, and no paint matches.

No, Mack couldn't rely on Blake and his squad. He needed to get something on Somerton himself. And to get it, he needed Teddy. If Somerton was in something deep enough that he'd taken out a contract on Teddy, it had to be something big enough to be found...with a little digging. Mack also hoped that whatever it was, it was something criminal, something that could put Alan Somerton away for a long time.

Mack opened the car door. He pocketed the keys and drew the edges of his jacket together against the cold. Down the street, a few remnant Christmas lights were still strung, blinking their colors through the night. But Mack barely glanced at them as he headed to the house—the house where he'd find Teddy.

"DON'T LET HIM IN, Holly. Please." Teddy released the blind on the front window. It snapped back into place, and she turned to her friend before Holly could unlatch the door.

"Teddy, don't be ridiculous. You have to talk to him."

"I can't." Up until the doorbell had rung, she'd believed she might actually be able to talk to Mack...one day. And then he was there, at Holly's front door. The sight of him—standing on the stoop in his black leather bomber jacket, his back to the door and his hands tucked into his pockets, snow lightly dusting his jet black hair—filled Teddy with a flood of emotions she couldn't begin to comprehend.

"I can't talk to him, Holly."

"Well, I'm certainly not going to leave him out there. For God's sake, Teddy, he's seen the lights, he knows we're home. And besides, your Jeep's in the driveway."

Holly started to unlock the door. Bogie was already wagging his tail, and Teddy wanted to call the malamute back, to demand he stay and not lavish such a forgiving welcome on Mack. But she was too late. In a second, Bogie had wriggled his bulk through the doorway, a virtual missile of excitement.

When Holly ushered Mack inside, he was smiling, obviously amused at Bogie's greeting. The second he lifted his gaze from the malamute to Teddy, however, his smile fell.

"Teddy."

She couldn't say his name. She couldn't even hold his dark stare that threatened to swallow her whole. Suddenly the front hall of Holly's house seemed far too close, the air too heavy. She wasn't ready for this.

"You must be Mack." Holly's voice sliced through the awkward silence, calm and cool.

Teddy saw Mack accept Holly's handshake.

"Holly Ryan," she introduced herself, perhaps realizing that Teddy was not about to.

"Mack Carlino." And then he gave Holly that smile—that charismatic, mysterious, dark-eyed smile—and Teddy knew Holly had just become another victim to Mack's charm.

"Teddy's told me...a lot about you, Mack."

"I'm sure she has." His smile faltered again when he looked to Teddy.

"Well, I'm going to make some tea...or something," Holly offered. "I think you two probably have some things to discuss. Come on, Bogie."

This time Teddy did not avoid Mack's stare. As she listened to Holly's receding footsteps, she held his steady gaze, unwilling to back down. Even as he brushed the snow from his hair and shrugged off his jacket, he didn't take his eyes off her.

"Teddy—"

"I have nothing to say to you, Mack."

She clenched her jaw, biting back sudden tears. She wouldn't let him see her cry, couldn't let him see the effect his closeness had on her.

"Then don't, Teddy. Just listen. Just let me explain."

"There's no need to explain." She shook her head.

"Teddy." He reached for her, but the second his cool fingers touched her cheek, she recoiled.

She took one step back, and turned to walk into the living room. He was right behind her.

"Teddy, you have to hear me out."

"Why, Mack? Why should I? So you can feed me a few more lies?"

"No. No more lies."

"Look, whatever you came here to tell me, I'm really not interested, okay? You're wasting your breath. So maybe you should just—"

Suddenly, his hands clamped onto her arms, and when he spun her around, she was so startled by the intensity of his expression, that she didn't even attempt to free herself.

"Mack, I'm not ready for this."

"Then you'd damn well better get ready."

"Mack—"

"No, Teddy, you're going to listen to me." He shook her when she tried to break free, his fingers digging into the soft flesh of her arms, and Teddy wondered if she'd find bruises there tomorrow.

"It's not me who's in danger," he said darkly. "Do you understand? It's you, Teddy. Someone is trying to kill *you.*"

14

"YOU'RE INSANE!"

Teddy tore herself from his grasp and drew away from him, as though needing to put space between herself and the truth. Or, more likely, between herself and him, Mack thought as he watched her face pale in disbelief.

"Teddy, so help me God, I'm not lying to you. You have to believe me."

She studied him, no doubt searching for something that would assure her his intentions were honest. Mack had expected her suspicion, and he certainly wouldn't blame her if she didn't believe he was telling the truth this time. But he prayed that she would.

Her eyes glistened with tears—tears that Mack knew she wouldn't dare shed in front of him. Teddy's stubbornness would never allow her to reveal to him how much he'd really hurt her.

"I told you someone was after me so that you would come with me, Teddy. So that you would leave Birdseye. I wasn't even a hundred percent sure of what was going on, but I figured if I told you *you* were the real target, that you'd get it into your head to stay and fight. I wouldn't have been able to protect you."

"I don't believe you."

"Teddy—"

"How do I know that this isn't just another lie? Another

story to get me to come with you again? So you can...*protect* me."

Her meaning behind the cutting emphasis of the word was clear to Mack. He knew she was referring to their love-making at the motel last night.

"Teddy." He placed his hands on her shoulders, and felt her flinch. But then her whole body seemed to slacken, and she allowed him to usher her to the couch.

When he sat beside her, Mack wanted to take her hands into his, to place a reassuring kiss on those trembling lips. But he didn't. He gave Teddy the physical space she seemed to need.

"I know I hurt you, Teddy," he said. "And I don't expect you ever to forgive me for that. But that's not why I'm here. Right now I really need you to believe me...in spite of everything that's happened."

She didn't avert her gaze, and in her shimmering gray eyes Mack could see her distrust.

"The bullet at the cabin, it was meant for you. Yesterday morning when you found me in the kitchen, I was checking the angle of the shot. And later, I went outside and saw the tracks the shooter had made. He was aiming for you, Teddy. Not me. And then there was the Jimmy."

"Both of us could have been killed."

"Yes, but *you* were the prime target. There isn't anyone with a vendetta against me, Teddy. Nobody would have tracked me all the way up to Birdseye on a case."

He saw her stiffen slightly at the mention of his "case."

"Teddy, the police are already searching for the guy who drove that Jimmy. I got a partial license number when he tried to run us off the road, and my ex-partner, Blake, ran it through the system. They're looking for a guy named Shel-don Wagner."

"I don't know anyone by that name. Why would someone I've never even heard of be trying to kill me?"

"Because he's been hired."

"Like...a hit man?" She released a nervous laugh. "Come on, Mack, even *I'm* not that gullible. Who would hire a—?"

"Your fiancé."

"Alan?" She shook her head. "No. No way, Mack. Not Alan. Now I *know* you're insane. There is no way—"

"Teddy, think about it. I know that you've already guessed Alan hired me to locate you. I was supposed to find you and report back to him. I thought that was it. I had no idea that he'd been using me as his bloodhound, to locate you and lay a trail for Wagner."

She was still shaking her head.

"Teddy, it took me a week to find you. No one else knew where you were. No one else could have found you. It was me. *I* was the one who brought Wagner to your doorstep. It was *my* trail he followed up to Birdseye. And the only person who knew I was looking for you was the man who hired me. It was Alan."

Mack couldn't begin to imagine what was going through Teddy's mind right now. The idea that someone she loved, or at least someone who she'd been ready to marry, had taken out a contract on her... God, how he wanted to take her in his arms and ease the anxiety, the pain and the confusion that he saw in her face as she grappled with the horrible truth. But then, wasn't he partly responsible for the hurt he saw there?

"But why?" she asked at last, her voice wavering.

"I don't know, Teddy. That's what we have to find out."

She let out a long trembling breath and got up from the couch. With one hand clutching her stomach as though she might be sick, Teddy paced the length of the living room several times. When she stopped at last, she stood with her back to him, facing the fireplace. He wondered if she was crying.

But when he crossed the room, moving behind her to settle his hands on her slim shoulders and turning her gently, Mack wasn't surprised to see that her eyes were dry.

"Teddy, it's the truth. You have to trust me on this."

She said nothing, only held his stare. Mack was certain that he saw a glimmer of belief. But it wasn't enough.

He took his wallet from his back pocket and pulled out one of Blake's official DPD cards.

"If you don't believe me, then call Blake...Detective Tennyson with the Denver Police Department."

She accepted the card, looking at it as she held it in one shaky hand.

"Teddy, for God's sake, you have to believe me. Your life could depend on it. And if anything happened to you..."

No. He wasn't going to let it get personal. He'd promised himself that. Keeping Teddy alive was his primary goal right now.

She lifted her gaze from the card, and handed it back to him. There was renewed determination on her face.

"So what do we do?" she asked.

Mack returned the card to his wallet. "We have to go back to Denver. At least by morning. We need to find evidence against Alan. But I can't do that without you, Teddy."

She nodded, and met his gaze briefly. He reached for her, sliding his arms around her waist and drawing her toward him. He was dying to hold her, to feel her body press against his as urgently as it once had, to know that everything could be right between them.

But he should have known it couldn't be that easy.

He heard Teddy's breath hitch, and she pulled away.

When she looked at him again, Mack saw the subtle clenching of a muscle along her jaw. But that was the only display of emotion from her. Everything else was locked deep inside. And Mack could only hope that Teddy would turn to him when she finally let loose all those emotions.

Right now, he doubted the likelihood of that ever happening. He'd lost Teddy's trust. Quite possibly forever. And the idea that he might never again hold her in his arms drove a pain into his heart greater than any he'd ever experienced.

TEDDY WATCHED the headlights of a car wash over the ceiling of Holly's guest bedroom. She'd been lying awake for what felt like hours, but the digital readout of the clock on the nightstand proved it had been no more than two.

It was past midnight.

She wondered if Mack was having better luck on the couch in the other room. Or if he was tossing and turning as she was.

She'd gone to bed early, shortly after her talk with Mack. She'd needed space from him. Time to think.

She'd lain awake, thinking about Alan, then Mack, and then Alan again. The idea that he might have hired someone to kill her…it was inconceivable. She'd been engaged to the man. They'd known each other two years. She'd worked with him, shared his bed, planned a future with him. Surely she should have guessed if he was capable of something so evil—hiring a hit man to kill his own fiancée.

It made no sense.

Yet, in spite of all his previous lies, instinct told Teddy that Mack was telling the truth. Or at least, he *believed* it was the truth.

Maybe he was wrong. Maybe it wasn't Alan.

Right, she berated herself, just like the way she'd hoped that the photograph in Mack's pocket had been a mistake. Who was she trying to kid?

Teddy watched another set of headlights sweep the ceiling. She closed her eyes, wishing for sleep, but her thoughts were too loud.

So, what if Mack was right, and Alan *had* hired someone to kill her...why? Why could Alan possibly want her dead?

It had to do with her last afternoon at Logan Publishing, Teddy was sure of it. Alan had thought she'd seen something on his computer. His rage had been completely irrational. But why? It wasn't entirely out of place for Alan to be looking at the company's private accounts, even before the year's end. So why had he been so defensive?

Mack was right. They had to check. And if nothing else, she had to show Mack that he was wrong. Alan wouldn't have...*couldn't* have hired someone to kill her. No, her love for Alan was gone, but she still couldn't believe him capable of that.

Teddy opened her eyes. She'd never sleep. And a part of her actually considered heading to Denver right now. In the middle of the night. Sneaking into Logan Publishing and getting to the bottom of this mess before the break of day.

Instead, she threw back the covers and reached for the robe Holly had given her. Tying it loosely around her waist, she opened the door and quietly stepped into the hallway. She needed a glass of milk. Or water. Anything.

She padded down the short corridor and stepped into the living room. In the pale moonlight that slipped through the partially open blinds, she could make out Mack's sleeping form on the couch. She stepped closer, and paused, watching the thin shafts of light touch his face.

He needed a shave, she thought, and almost smiled as she remembered the first time she'd laid eyes on him. In the bar that night. All rugged handsomeness, the mysterious dark stranger. And then the next morning, standing over her, a few hours after he'd undressed her and put her to bed.

It was only days ago, and yet it felt like a lifetime. In that short time, she'd come to know Mack better than she knew Alan. Or had she? She thought she'd known Alan well enough to marry him, and now chances were he was trying to have her killed. She thought she'd known Mack, but how much of what she knew about him was truth and how much lies?

All of a sudden, she wanted to touch Mack, to have him touch her, as though being with him could offer some answers. It was a ridiculous notion. She knew that. After everything that had happened, she'd be twice a fool to rush into his arms now. But at the same time, Teddy couldn't help thinking that if Mack made love to her again, she might somehow know what he truly felt for her. Because nothing had felt more honest than their lovemaking.

No! The very thought of sleeping with Mack again was absurd. He'd betrayed her. He'd lied to her and deceived her. And for all she knew, the only reason he'd slept with her was to stay close to his case. She'd so willingly accepted Mack's word that Alan had hired him only to find her. But what if there was more behind Alan's hiring a PI? What if Mack had been contracted to find something? She'd suspected him of searching her papers earlier, up at the cabin. And what if, in his "search," he figured he had to get close to her? Sleep with her?

God! She didn't know what to believe anymore!

Angrily, she swiped a hand through her hair and started for the kitchen.

"Don't leave, Teddy."

Mack's voice startled her.

"Teddy, please." His whisper sent a shudder of familiar longing through her.

"I'm sorry. I didn't mean to wake you. I was just getting a glass of water."

"You didn't wake me." He rolled over, catching her gaze. "I want to tell you something."

"Mack, I—"

"Teddy, just listen."

Even with his face in partial shadow, Teddy could see the sincerity in his expression. God, how could she still love him?

He propped himself up on his elbows and nodded, as though inviting her to join him. But when Teddy moved to the couch, she perched herself instead on the edge of the coffee table and faced him. On the side table next to him, she saw the dim glint of moonlight on Mack's gun—a cold reminder that he could be right, that someone might be after her, and that Mack intended to be her protector.

"Teddy, I want to explain about what happened in Birdseye. At the cabin."

"You don't have to explain anything, Mack."

"Yes, I do. You have to know what my intentions were. No matter what you think of me now, I want you to know the truth about what happened up there."

He leaned closer, and the sheet slipped from his chest. Seeing the strong line of his jaw, and the outline of his lips, Teddy recalled the heat of his kiss even now.

"Alan hired me to find you. That's it. It was supposed to be a simple case. I spent a week following your trail, looking everywhere for you, before I ended up at Sly's Tavern. But even before I laid eyes on you, Teddy, I knew that I couldn't turn you in. Not until I'd heard your side of the story. Something didn't feel right about it. That's why I followed you, and that's why I knew where the cabin was, your name, everything."

He reached over and took Teddy's hand in his. Immediately, she felt a familiar desire lick through her, and she remembered those very hands on her body, holding her, caressing her, touching her in ways she'd never been touched before.

"When I found you, I intended nothing more than to talk to you," Mack continued, his low voice barely a whisper. "I didn't call Alan because I wanted to be sure about what I would be doing to you if I did. That was it, Teddy. I never expected to fall in love with you. I didn't mean for it to happen, and I tried everything to stop it."

He caressed the back of her hand for a long moment.

"I never wanted to lie to you. But if you'd known why I was in Birdseye in the first place... I didn't know how to tell you, Teddy. Not without losing you. I know there's nothing I can say now that will change things. And I don't expect you to forgive me."

"Mack—"

"No, Teddy. Just let me say this." He drew her to him, guiding her to the couch so that she was sitting in the juncture of his thighs. And when he lifted a hand to her cheek to caress her lips with his thumb, Teddy thought she would cry. She wanted so badly to be with Mack. To love him the way she had. To trust him again, with her life, with her body and soul.

"I just want to say one thing," he whispered. "Whatever happens and whatever you may think of me, I want you to know that I *do* love you, Teddy."

She knew she was going to kiss him, in spite of the voice in her head that reminded her of how she'd been hurt. Mack was too close, his power over her too strong. She couldn't deny it.

He moved toward her, closing the small gap between them. His own desire seemed to unfold like an invisible cape, wrapping itself around her and drawing her into his kiss. His hands took her face, cradling it gently. Strong fingers fanned back through her hair, bringing her ever closer, until she could feel the heat of his bare chest through the sheer material of her robe.

And when his lips brushed hers, she was surprised at tenderness in Mack's kiss. She'd expected him to take her with all the passion that had driven them together before, at the cabin and at the motel. But this time there was a hesitancy behind the touching of his lips on hers, a deep affection that touched her heart.

Even as his wide hands slid down her shoulders and along her back, settling on her hips, Teddy was surprised at the restraint he seemed to be exercising. She could feel the quickening of his pulse and still his kiss was careful and deliberate.

He was leaving it up to her, Teddy realized. He was letting her decide how far she was willing to trust him this time, how much of herself she dared give him. And a part of her wanted everything she knew Mack was capable of—she wanted to feel those deft hands all over her, she wanted to feel his lips burn along her skin, she wanted to feel the power of his body surround her, consume her, and move inside her. She wanted him to drive away all her doubts with his love, the kind of love that had woken her from her old life and shown her a new one.

But another part of her clung to those doubts. The part that had been hurt; the part that could no longer hold back the tears.

"Teddy?"

He must have felt the small sobs that shuddered through her even as she'd answered his kiss. He drew back, trying to see her face. But Teddy was concentrating on their joined hands in her lap.

"Mack, I'm sorry. I...I can't do this."

"I understand." His fingertips were cool against her cheek as he wiped at the tears there.

She dared to look into his eyes, afraid she would see disappointment, but found only compassion.

"It's just...everything's so confusing right now. With Alan, and—"

"Teddy, shh." He pulled her into his embrace, wrapping his comforting arms around her, and rocking her.

And as she held on to him, as she clung to his strength and his warmth, she heard him whisper, "It's all right, Teddy. Everything will be all right. And whatever you decide, I'll understand."

15

TEDDY HAD BROKEN most of the speed limits between Fort Collins and Denver, but Mack didn't seem to have any difficulty keeping up. They'd taken both cars, Mack following her in case they were tailed. At eight o'clock on a Sunday morning, however, the southbound traffic on the Interstate 25 was minimal. They would have easily spotted a red Jimmy, or any other vehicle for that matter.

Over a hurried breakfast in Fort Collins, Mack had instructed Holly to tell no one that they'd been there. If Detective Tennyson called, she should inform him of their trip to Logan Publishing. Other than that, there had been very little breakfast conversation, only a tense silence.

Teddy hadn't mentioned Mack's theory about Alan to Holly, nor had she told her friend exactly what they were up to this morning. She'd said her goodbyes with promises of calling Holly later, and she and Mack had gone to their respective vehicles.

Since then, Teddy drove ahead, keeping an eye on Mack behind her and remembering the last time she'd seen his lights in the Jeep's rearview mirror. During the hour drive to Denver, she'd relived in her mind almost every moment she'd shared with Mack, from the cabin to the motel and then last night.

He hadn't pushed her last night. His kiss, although fraught with longing, had not been insistent. He'd taken her into his arms and comforted her with complete disregard

for his own needs and desires, and it was Mack's selfless-
ness that had touched Teddy. As he'd held her in the solace
of his embrace, Teddy had actually allowed herself, for a
brief time, to entertain thoughts of a future with Mack.

She'd taken those thoughts back to bed with her, after
leaving him on the couch, and had lain awake for several
more hours, searching for answers. But none came. And until they figured out what Alan was up to, Teddy could not
trust any decision she made.

She slowed the Jeep at the Stillson Avenue entrance to the
parking garage of Logan Publishing, and checked her rearview mirror again. Mack was right behind her, turning into
the dark concrete structure and following her around each
corner and ramp to the Visitor's parking on the lower level.
He'd suggested they leave the cars someplace other than
where Teddy normally parked so that no one would know
they were there.

The level was empty. Teddy locked the Jeep, leaving Bogie in the back, and walked to Mack's car, her boots echoing
through the cavernous space. He must have recognized her
trepidation when he joined her, because he reached over
and took her hand, giving it an encouraging squeeze.

"Are you ready?"

Teddy nodded, finding strength from his grip, and led
him to the elevators.

Wordlessly she entered her passcode into the keypad
mounted between the two sets of stainless-steel doors, and
after a few moments one set shuddered open. Even in the
close quarters of the elevator, standing shoulder to shoulder, watching each passing floor light up in the column of
buttons, they said nothing.

And in their silence, Teddy was certain she felt Mack's
tension as distinctly as she felt her own. During the drive,
her mind had been so preoccupied with Mack and with try-

ing to sort out her feelings for him, that she hadn't entirely comprehended what it was they were about to do.

Not that they'd discussed it much, either. In fact, neither of them really knew what they were looking for.

It was then that Teddy wondered if Alan might be up-stairs already. Her stomach lurched at the thought. It wouldn't be unlike Alan to come in on a Sunday morning. She should have thought of that earlier. It would have been smart to drive past his parking spot on their way down to the lower level, to make sure that his Jag wasn't there.

"It's going to be all right, Teddy." Mack squeezed her hand again, obviously sensing her fears. And when she looked up into his reassuring smile, she wondered if he wanted to kiss her as much as she did him at that moment. "Trust me," he said, just as the doors slid open.

Stepping off the elevator and into the thirty-eighth-floor lobby of Logan Publishing was like stepping into another world. She'd been removed from all of its chrome-and-marble grandeur for so long that it seemed as if she was walking through a dream instead of what had been her life for so many years.

But within seconds, Teddy *was* home. Leading Mack through the hushed lobby, past the empty receptionist's command center, and to the corridor beyond, Teddy was overcome with a sudden pride and fierce defensiveness. This was her family's place. *Her* place. It was what her father had worked years for. And if Mack was right, if Alan was up to something corrupt involving Logan Publishing, she would be the one to bring him down. *No* one would steal the Logan legacy.

Halfway along the main corridor and to the right was Alan's office. Teddy took the corner cautiously, with Mack behind her. And when she saw Alan's closed door, she let out a tense breath. Alan always left his door open if he was in. They were lucky.

"This way," she murmured to Mack, wondering why she was whispering. She had every right to be here, she thought as she reached for the security number-pad beside the polished teak door that bore Alan's nameplate.

She keyed in her passcode and waited for the green light to flash on. Nothing. Only the solid red indicator at the top of the panel.

Maybe she'd made a mistake. She was nervous. Her fingers were shaking. She must have hit a wrong key.

Teddy tried it again.

Still the red light shone.

"It's not working, Mack."

"What isn't?"

"My passcode. It's not working."

"Could he have changed it?"

"I suppose so. But why would he, unless..." She didn't have to finish. They both knew that if Alan had restricted the password to his office it could mean only one thing—there *was* something he was hiding.

"Just relax, Teddy, and try it again."

"I already tried it twice. If I try a third time and it's wrong, the system will notify security and they'll be up here in a flash."

"So? It's your company."

"Yes, but security would also inform Alan at home, since it's his office. They'd call him even before they come up here to investigate. We can't get in, Mack. Not without alerting him of our presence."

Mack exhaled loudly and Teddy watched him pace the width of the hall. "So what now? We've got to get in there, Teddy. If we have to go through all the red tape of a search warrant, Alan will have the time he needs to destroy the evidence. And then we've got nothing on him."

"Come on." Teddy caught Mack's hand in hers. "Follow me. There's another way in...I hope."

SHE LED HIM around the corner and down several hallways before stopping at a set of wide double doors that spanned the full width of the corridor. Mack wondered why he should be surprised to see Teddy's name in gold-plated brass.

She entered her passcode into the keypad, and this time she was rewarded with a green light. She swung open one of the doors to a flood of sunshine, and as Mack stepped inside he was struck by the vastness of the office. Teddy was already behind the massive mahogany desk that extended the length of the raised section at the room's west side, and as she switched on her computer, Mack let his gaze rove over the posh furnishings and decor.

This was the *real* Teddy Logan.

That fact hit home the moment they'd stepped off the elevator and into the lobby. Surrounded by the opulence of Logan Publishing, Mack was abruptly reminded of the vast contrast between his life and Teddy's. She'd been born into this world of luxury and wealth, and she fit it to a tee—classy, refined, elegant.

The woman he'd fallen in love with, up in a remote mountain cabin, didn't seem to belong in this world of chrome and glass, marble and mahogany. She'd seemed so comfortable with the simpler life. And yet, looking at her now, in her own surroundings, he could still see a part of the Teddy he'd first met. Perhaps it was the fact that she wore jeans and her Gore-Tex parka instead of some high-power business suit that he suspected she usually wore when sitting in that tall leather chair.

He stood next to her, planting his hands on the edge of the desk as he watched her long fingers fly across the keyboard. His gaze lifted, stopping on the framed photographs at the head of her desk—photos of Teddy and Alan Somerton together, happy in each other's arms.

"It'll take a couple seconds to log in," she told him, and eased back into her chair as she waited.

But Mack couldn't take his eyes off the photographs, imagining the two of them together, imagining Teddy in Somerton's arms, in his bed...the man who wanted her dead. The very thought twisted a cold knife of hatred in Mack's heart.

Teddy must have followed his gaze, because after a momentary silence, she reached across the desk and tipped the two frames over, laying them facedown.

Without a word, she placed her hand over his and let it linger there briefly before turning back to the keyboard.

"What are you doing?" Mack asked her eventually as he tried to grasp the computer jargon that flashed across the screen.

"I'm breaking into Alan's system."

"You can do that?"

"Uh-huh."

"Aren't there passwords?"

"I know his password. I set it all up for him."

"What if he changed it, like he changed his entry code?"

"Alan's not exactly a computer whiz. I taught him everything he knows about the Logan system. He manages to work within it well enough, but has no idea how to manipulate it."

Mack watched her, knowing that there was no way for him to comprehend the multitude of layers she delved into as she went farther and farther into the system. Beeps sounded and on-screen messages flashed, and still Teddy typed furiously.

"I'm in," she announced at last.

"You're into Alan's system?"

She nodded. "His records and personal files. We keep everything on a mainframe here."

"So now what? What are you looking for?"

Columns of numbers raced across the screen. "I'm looking at the corporate and private accounts."

For several long minutes, he stood behind Teddy, leaning over her shoulder as she scanned countless screens of numbers and on-line spreadsheets. But none of it made any sense to Mack. All he knew now was that if there *was* anything to be found out about Somerton through his computer files, Teddy would find it.

He only prayed that there was something to be found.

And then he heard Teddy's quick gasp of disbelief.

She shook her head. "Oh, God. I...I don't believe this."

"What, Teddy? What is it?"

"These accounts...they're all wrong."

"How wrong?"

"Really wrong. There's money missing...lots of money. None of these figures make any sense, unless... Mack, he's...he's been milking these accounts for months. Cleaning them right out. He's been moving funds to outside sources all over the place, out-of-state, overseas. I don't believe this."

"It's called embezzlement, Teddy."

"I know what it's called," she snapped, but Mack knew her anger wasn't directed at him. He placed a hand on her shoulder and massaged it gently, hoping to ease her rage.

"How much is it?" he asked.

"Right now...at a glance, I can't say for certain, but there must be close to a couple million. The son of a bitch..."

She hit another series of keys and kept scanning.

"So can you save these files, Teddy? Copy them onto a disk or something? We don't want Alan wiping out every last shred of evidence."

Teddy nodded. "I'm already doing that, Mack."

She hammered at the keyboard, her eyes glued to the screen.

"Once I've downloaded them onto my system, I can—"

A shrill beep cut her off.

Teddy swore, and instantly her hands froze over the keyboard. She stared at the screen, removed her hands and shrank back from the computer.

"Teddy? What is it? What's happened?" Mack looked at the computer screen and saw the warning message flash across the columns of figures: *Log-in attempt unsuccessful.*

"He's here."

"Who's here? Alan? He's here now?"

Teddy nodded, staring wide-eyed at the red warning message.

"Where, Teddy?"

"He just tried to log on. And it's definitely local."

ALAN SOMERTON stared at his computer monitor.

User already logged on.

Again he tried his password. Again the message.

As a cold realization settled over him, he looked from the screen to the photo beside his terminal.

"Teddy." He whispered her name, the sound almost gentle. But there was nothing gentle about the way his hand shot out to snatch the framed photograph and smash it against the office wall. There was an explosion of shattered glass, and then an ear-ringing silence.

He imagined he could hear her in her office right now, even though distance made that impossible.

And he knew it was Teddy. She was the only person who knew his password. She was the only one would think to break into his files.

Alan stood from the desk, sending his chair spinning backward on its wheels, and unlocked the top drawer. When he threw it open, the revolver inside slammed against the rear panel with a loud thud.

He reached for it, and checked the cylinder. As he headed to the door, his fingers tightened around the walnut grip.

"TEDDY, does Alan have a gun?" Mack unclipped his holster. He stood behind Teddy where she refused to budge from her computer, madly typing in the commands that would copy the incriminating files from Alan's system to hers.

"Teddy," he asked again. "Does Alan own a gun?"

"No."

"Are you sure?"

She spared him a quick glance. "Mack, when it comes to Alan, I'm hardly the one you should ask about being sure."

"Fine. Listen, we've got to get out of here."

"No, Mack. I need these files. Without them we've got no proof. Just two more minutes."

"Teddy, he's got to know you're here. You can't stay."

"Just two more minutes, Mack."

"We don't *have* two minutes."

Mack looked at the partly open door of Teddy's office. Almost a minute had passed since the warning message had first flashed across the screen. If Alan knew Teddy was in his system, then he could be here any second.

And there was no way Mack was about to leave her alone in the office so he could go searching for Alan in the labyrinth of corridors. No, all he could do for now was lock the door so Teddy could finish downloading the files. Then he'd call Blake for backup.

Mack didn't make it to the other side of the office. His heart froze when he spotted the snub-nosed barrel of the revolver inch around the edge of the door and level directly on Teddy.

"Teddy!" he shouted, scrambling toward the door. "Teddy, get down!"

Mack lunged for the revolver.

But he was too late.

An ear-shattering shot ripped through the office a split second before Mack's shoulder collided with the door. He heard a startled gasp as Alan's arm was momentarily pinned between the door and its frame, and the revolver dropped to the floor.

Mack was vaguely aware of footsteps running down the corridor, and then voices. It looked as if the cavalry had come to their rescue.

He spun around toward the desk but he couldn't see Teddy. In that moment, the room reeled into slow motion.

"Teddy! Oh, God, Teddy!"

He staggered across the office, panic coursing through him.

"Teddy!"

He pushed his way behind the desk, and when he saw her on the floor, his heart stopped.

"Teddy."

Then she moved. She straightened up, looking at Mack with wide eyes, her face almost white with shock.

"Teddy, are you all right?"

She only nodded as he helped her up.

"Are you hurt?"

"No." Her lips mouthed the word, but no sound came out.

"Come on, sit down." Mack started to guide her to the chair she had sat in only seconds ago, but when he spun it around, Teddy stopped. She reached out one shaky hand to the back of the chair, and Mack saw her fingers flutter across the ragged hole left by a bullet. If Mack hadn't yelled his warning...

"Teddy." He took her by the shoulders forcing her to look at him and not the bullet hole that marked her close brush with death. "Are you sure you're all right?"

"I'm fine, Mack." She straightened, and he felt her shoulders go rigid. She was determined to be strong, in spite of the shock he knew gripped her.

The voices in the corridor grew louder.

"Stay here, all right?" he told her before he headed to the closed door.

When Mack stepped out of the office, there were at least a half dozen uniformed officers in the hall. Then he saw Alan, already being cuffed, and Blake standing nearby.

Blake gave him a nod from across the corridor, and turned to the nearest officer. "Read him his rights, will ya?" Blake elbowed his way through the officers toward Mack, and when he joined him at the door, he waved a piece of paper.

"Arrest warrant," he explained with a tired grin.

"How did you manage that so fast?"

"Sheldon Wagner. Our boys picked him up at a bar brawl, of all things, 2:00 a.m. this morning. Four hours in interview and he finally gave it up. Copped a plea with the D.A. and gave us Somerton. You should have seen old Judge Myers's face when we woke him up for this warrant. Anyway, when we didn't find Somerton at his residence, we came straight here. And a damned good thing we did, it looks like."

Mack nodded, looking past Blake's shoulder to where the

arresting officer turned Alan around. The look on Somerton's face was one Mack had seen hundreds of times during just as many arrests—a frantic look, somewhere between incredulity and defeat, and laced with quiet rage. But this time there seemed more rage than anything. And it was directed at Mack.

"And you must be Ms. Logan?" he heard Blake ask.

Mack turned. At some point, Teddy had stepped out of the office. He hadn't been aware of her behind him, but she was there now, at his side. He wondered how much she'd heard. But she didn't seem concerned with anything involving Sheldon Wagner. Her steady gaze was fixed on Alan, her face awash with shock and disbelief.

Mack reached down and took her hand in his. Her stance eased, but only marginally.

"Are you all right, Ms. Logan?" Blake asked her. "We heard a shot."

"Yes." She managed to drag her stare from Alan long enough to answer Blake. "Yes, thank you. I'm fine, Detective—"

"Tennyson. Blake Tennyson."

"Ah." Teddy accepted his handshake and Mack was surprised to see the wavering smile that struggled to her lips. "I should have guessed," she said, gesturing to her own eye in an indication of Blake's patch. "It's good to meet you, Blake."

But Mack could see that the pleasantries were far from easy for her, and he wished she and Blake had been able to meet under better circumstances.

"I hate to ask this of you, Ms. Logan—"

"Teddy."

"Teddy," Blake repeated. "I hate to ask, but I'm going to need you downtown for a statement."

She nodded, her eyes once again locking onto Alan's.

"I'll bring her," Mack offered.

"That'll be fine. I'll see you guys later then." Blake turned, leaving them in the doorway.

When Mack looked at Teddy, her jaw was clenched tight as she held Alan's stare from across the corridor. Mack couldn't imagine what she was going through right now. It wasn't bad enough that the man she'd intended to marry had hired someone to kill her. He'd tried to kill her *himself*.

In the icy stare that passed between Teddy and Somerton, Mack guessed it would take her some time to get over the shock.

He started to put an arm around her shoulder, intending to support her, but he felt Teddy stiffen. No, she wanted to stand on her own, he realized. She needed to.

There was a proud tilt to her chin as she watched the officers usher Alan down the corridor. And when Alan called out her name, Teddy remained motionless. Speechless.

Only once the last officer had left and Blake had given Mack a parting nod, did Teddy turn to him at last.

"Thank you, Mack." She remained at arm's length, but he knew why. He could see the tears welling in her eyes. "Thank you for...saving my life."

"You don't have to thank me, Teddy." He lifted a hand to caress her cheek, and when she pressed her lips into his palm, Mack felt that deep ache in his chest again.

"Are you going to be all right?" He didn't know why he'd asked the question. He knew she would be. In time.

Teddy nodded. She took his hand and gave him a smile. Nothing more. She didn't kiss him. Nor did she fall into his embrace. There were other things she had to deal with first. Mack understood that, as much as it pained him.

And until then, he would pray every day that Teddy would find her way back into his arms.

_____Epilogue_____

MACK POCKETED the keys for his rental car, and took the stairs to his office two at a time even though he was bone-tired.

Friday morning.

Eleven days and eighteen hours, and he hadn't heard a word from Teddy.

He'd taken her to headquarters for her statement late that morning almost two weeks ago, and had driven her home afterward. In the car, outside the Logan estate, she'd said nothing, only leaned over and given him a brief but heartfelt kiss. Then she was gone. He'd waited as she and Bogie crossed the driveway, and he watched the long embrace she gave her father on the front step before they disappeared inside.

That was the last Mack had seen of her. He'd followed the stories in the _Denver Post_, had known of the judge's denial for bail, and had finally read about Somerton's unforeseen confession.

Mack had tried to lose himself in his work. His caseload over the past week and a half had certainly been enough to keep him going sixteen hours a day or longer. Busy enough that he still hadn't made arrangements to retrieve his Mustang from Birdseye, but not busy enough, by far, to keep his mind off Teddy. Not an hour had gone by that Mack didn't think about calling her. And not five minutes had gone by without him imagining her in his arms again. Every time he dreamed, she was there with him. Every time he closed his eyes, he could see her smile.

Even now, as Mack reached the top landing and started down the long corridor to his office, he cursed his memories. Above the stale odor of the old building, the musty floorboards and the old plaster, he could almost believe he smelled Teddy's perfume... He closed his eyes, and groaned. How long did it take to get over someone? How long before the ache was gone?

It was the faint tinkle of dog tags that broke his thoughts and stopped him in his tracks.

"Bogie?"

The overgrown malamute barreled down the narrow hallway toward him, but it was past the charging dog that Mack's attention was riveted.

She sat on the floor, her long, slender legs drawn into the circle of her arms, her chin resting on her knees, and that golden-blond hair swept so casually over one shoulder.

Mack was certain he'd forgotten how to breathe when Teddy smiled at him.

He watched her stand. Her Gore-Tex jacket hung open, and under it she wore a turtleneck and a wool sweater over her leggings, but Mack had no problem imagining every enticing and memorized curve beneath that heavy sweater.

Her smile never faltered. Mack couldn't remember if he'd ever seen anything more beautiful. Even as he petted Bogie's head and stumbled around the big dog, Mack couldn't take his eyes off Teddy. And when he stood before her at last, breathing in the arousing familiarity of her scent, he wasn't at all certain what to say to her. He'd be happy enough just to stand there and stare, he realized.

Teddy, fortunately, made the first move. In one graceful motion, she took his hands in hers and leaned toward him to place a gentle kiss on his cheek.

"How are you, Mack?" she asked, still holding his hands.

"I'm fine, I guess." He wondered if his shock was visible. "And you?"

"Good. Well...okay, you know?"

He nodded. It was going to take more than a couple of weeks for Teddy to come to terms with what Alan had done to her.

"I'm...I'm sorry I haven't called."

"I understand, Teddy."

She released his hands finally and managed a smile. "I was just...in the area and thought I'd stop by. See where you work."

"Right." He grinned at her attempted fib.

"Well, okay, so I wasn't in this *specific* area."

"Uh-huh."

"All right. I came all the way out here to see you," she admitted, her eyes sparkling with inner laughter. "I wanted to see you, Mack. I...I've missed you."

"That goes both ways, Teddy."

She nodded as a thoughtful smile curved her lips.

Mack played with his keys in one hand for a moment, uncertain what to suggest. After all, if he'd suggested what was *really* on his mind, they'd be going back to his place. Instead, he decided to slide the key in the lock.

"Would you like to come in? I can make some coffee or—"

"Actually, Mack, I can't."

"Oh."

"The thing is, I was kind of hoping you'd be up for more than coffee." She caught herself, perhaps seeing the quick gleam in Mack's eyes and realizing the implication of what she'd just said. "What I'm trying to say is, I was hoping you were maybe up for a drive. To Birdseye. I know you've probably already gone up and gotten your car, but my stuff's still there and I was wondering if you'd...come along with me."

"No, Teddy."

"No?" Disappointment clouded her smile.

"No. I mean, no I haven't gotten my car yet." He watched her expression ease again. "I've been so busy with cases that I haven't had a chance to make arrangements." But the truth was, he'd put it off for one reason—the thought of going to that cabin again, by himself, had been unbearable.

"So what do you say, Mack? First greasy spoon is on me."

"Oh, now if *that* isn't an invitation I can't turn down. You're on."

THE ROADS had been clear, and if Mack hadn't actually taken her up on her offer of lunch at a greasy spoon, they would have rolled into Birdseye in record time. By the time Teddy steered the Jeep into the driveway of Sly's cabin, she was dying to stretch her legs.

Not that the hours with Mack hadn't sailed by with the same ease as the breathtaking mountain winterscapes. Once they'd left the city limits behind them, the initial tension had worn off and they'd started talking. First about Alan. Mack had followed the case, but there were details to be filled in and Teddy did her best. She was surprised at how easy it was to talk about Alan now, or perhaps it was easy because it was Mack she was talking to. She didn't know.

She'd gone on to tell him about Logan Publishing—how she and her father were working together, repairing the damage Alan had done, and getting on with things. Getting on with life.

The same seemed true of Mack. He was taking on more and more cases. As he described for Teddy the hours of work he'd put in over the past week and a half, she couldn't help wondering if Mack had been using the same tactic she had, burying himself in his work so he would forget the time they'd shared. She wondered if the strategy had been successful for him—her *own* work certainly had done nothing to fill the emptiness where Mack had once been.

When they reached Sly's cabin, Teddy was reminded of that emptiness even more keenly. She took the keys from the Jeep's ignition and looked at the squat, snow-covered building. This place, she realized, was special to her. It always would be because it was here that she'd first discovered true love, that she'd first experienced Mack's love.

Mack, too, seemed speechless as they both stepped out of the Jeep and started toward the porch. Even Bogie seemed to have missed the place, Teddy thought as the dog romped through the deep snow.

"We probably shouldn't stay long, Teddy," Mack suggested. "It's fours hours back." But there was definite disappointment in his voice as he unlocked the cabin and stepped inside.

Teddy lingered in the open doorway. Seeing Mack move through the cabin, collecting their belongings, she was struck by her driving desire to be with him.

For almost two weeks she'd avoided Mack for this very reason. Ever since Alan, she'd been careful about listening to her heart, afraid to put faith in it again.

She'd stayed away from Mack as long as she could, testing herself, testing the ache she felt so deeply for him. She had tried to block her memories of him, but he'd been there, in her thoughts and in her heart, all the time. She thought she'd be able to stop thinking about him if he wasn't near her. But Mack, and her memories of him, had been the only things on her mind. And they were what had gotten her through the whole mess with Alan over the past week and a half.

"Teddy? What is it?" Mack had caught her staring, and

stopped in the middle of the front hall. That dark gaze of his locked onto hers, and Teddy couldn't escape it, even if she'd wanted to.

But she didn't. She wanted to lose herself in his gaze, lose herself in Mack's love all over again.

"What's wrong, Teddy?"

"Nothing." She shook her head, and the smile she gave him came straight from her heart. "I've missed this place."

She couldn't take her eyes off him, even as he walked toward her.

"I've missed you, Mack," she whispered. "I've missed *us*."

In his eyes, Teddy could see that he'd been waiting all day for this, longing for it as deeply as she had from the moment she'd seen him walking down that corridor toward his office this morning. When he reached up and took her face between his broad hands, cradling it to meet his kiss, Teddy could taste his passion before his mouth found hers. And when it did, when she first felt those wonderful lips press so urgently and hungrily against hers, Teddy felt her whole body come alive. It was as though Mack's kiss fed her the very part of life she'd been missing since she'd left him.

He brought one hand down to her waist, sliding it beneath her heavy sweater. A familiar longing washed through her as his cool fingers followed the line of her ribs, and her breath hitched when he cupped one breast in his strong hand.

Her own hands traveled downward, and she hooked her fingers around the waistband of his jeans, drawing his body tight against hers. Teddy smiled under his kiss as she ran her hand over the taut denim and caressed his already straining erection.

His lips left hers with a low moan, and when he burned kisses along the sensitive skin of her throat, she heard him murmur, "I've missed us, too, Teddy. I've been going crazy missing you."

If it hadn't been for Bogie barking just then, Teddy knew exactly where she and Mack would have ended up within a matter of seconds. With her body still pressed firmly against his, Teddy turned and looked out to the clearing where Bogie tossed a stick for himself and barked in the hopes of finding a playmate. But Teddy wasn't going anywhere. She leaned back and rested her head against the solidness of Mack's chest, and as he wrapped his arms around her, she was quite certain that she could stay in Mack's embrace for the rest of her life.

Bogie was definitely on his own.

"I wonder if Sly would consider selling this place," she said eventually, gazing out past the malamute to the frozen lake.

"Are you thinking you'd like to buy it?"

"Actually, yeah. As a getaway, you know? I'd like to see the lake in the summer. In fact, I'd like to see it all through the seasons. And...I'd like to see it with you, Mack."

"You would, would you?"

"Yeah." She smiled and tilted her head back so that he could give her a light kiss. When she turned in his arms at last, Teddy searched those dark eyes. It would take time for her to come to terms with Alan's betrayal, but there was little doubt in her mind as to Mack's love for her. In spite of the lies that had brought him into her arms, Teddy knew she could trust him. More than that, she knew she could trust her feelings for him.

"So do you think you could actually be happy with some poor Irish-Italian boy from New York?"

She traced her finger along the line of his firm lips and returned his smile. "Incredibly so," she answered him.

And when Mack swept her into his embrace this time—enveloping her in his tender passion—there was no denying her love for him either.

**Don't miss the red-hot sexy reads from
Temptation's® BLAZE**

Turn the page for a sneak preview of

Scandalized!

by
Lori Foster

Scandalized!

Lori Foster

Out of sheer necessity, he pulled the car off the main street and onto a small dirt road that led to a dead end. When Tony was younger, he and his brother had come here to make out with girls. In those days there was a wide cornfield, but it had been replaced by a small park with a street lamp. Obviously things had changed, but the premise was the same. Isolation.

Despite the fact that he was sweating, he left the car running, for it was a cold night in early November. He killed the lights, though, giving himself some illusionary concealment. When he turned to face her, he already had his mouth open to start his argument, but he was brought up short by the picture she presented.

Moonlight poured over her, revealing the sheen of

dark hair, the shape of her ears, her high arched brows. Her eyelashes left long feathery shadows on her cheeks and shielded her eyes from his gaze. Her hands were folded in her lap. She appeared somehow very unsure of herself...vulnerable. It wasn't a look he was used to, not from her. She lifted her gaze to his face, and once again he felt that deep frustration.

It wasn't that Olivia was beautiful. She was by far the most elegant woman he'd ever known, but she wasn't classically beautiful. He had dated more attractive women, made love to them, had long-standing affairs with them that had left him numb. But Olivia was the only woman whose personality, intelligence and disposition were attractive enough to entice him into asking her to carry his child. That was something. More than something, actually, when you figured it was usually looks that drew a man first, and the other, more important features of a woman that kept him drawn.

When he remained quiet, she said, "I know what I'm asking seems absurd. After all, you could have any woman you want, and after knowing you for so long, it's obvious you don't particularly want me. That's okay, because up until you mentioned your plan, I hadn't really thought about wanting you, either.

"But you see, I've made my career everything." Her hands twisted in her lap and her voice shook. "Just as you don't want any involvements now, neither do I. That's why the idea seems so perfect. I haven't taken the time or the effort to get to know very many men, and almost never on an intimate level. These days, only an idiot would indulge in casual sex. But starting a relationship isn't something I want, either. So I thought, maybe we could both get what we wanted."

Tony searched her face, feeling dumbfounded. Surely she wasn't suggesting what he thought she was. "I want a baby. What is it you want, Olivia?"

She turned her head away from him and looked out the window. Sounding so unlike herself, she whispered in a small voice, "I want a wild, hot, never-to-be-forgotten affair. For two weeks. If during that time I conceive, the baby will become yours, and we'll go on with the rest of your plans. If I don't conceive, I'll be on my way and you can find another woman who, hopefully, will prove more fertile. You won't owe me a thing.

* * *

Temptation® turns up the heat in BLAZE.
Look out for Scandalized!
by Lori Foster, available in July 1998

Spoil yourself next month
with these four novels from

THE HEARTBREAKER by Vicki Lewis Thompson

Mike Tremayne had just seen beautiful Beth Nightingale for the
first time in eight years and found her just as desirable as ever.
But Beth had no intention of falling for Mike again; after all he'd
already betrayed her twice, once when he became engaged to her
sister, and then again, when he walked out on both of them.

SCANDALIZED! by Lori Foster

Blaze

Tony Austin wanted a baby, not a lover. So he asked Olivia
Anderson to carry a baby for him. Little did he know that Olivia
had no intention of getting pregnant but she liked the idea of a
couple of nights of hot, *hot* sex with Tony! Then love got in the
way and upset both their plans...

HIS DOUBLE, HER TROUBLE by Donna Sterling

The Wrong Bed

Brianna Devon had planned an intimate party for two as a
surprise to celebrate Evan Rowland's return home. The surprise,
however, was on her. Too late she discovered she was in bed *not*
with her school sweetheart, but with his identical twin—her
nemesis Jake Rowland! *And* she'd enjoyed every minute of it!

THAT WILDER MAN by Susan Liepitz

As teenagers, Max Wilder and his girlfriend Liza Jane had a
wild time—in town and in bed. Now a richer and a wiser man,
Max had returned home. But he had no intention of giving her
another chance to break his heart because, years ago, Liza Jane
had run off and married his best friend...

On sale from 13th July 1998

SPOT THE DIFFERENCE

Spot all ten differences between the two pictures featured below and you could win a year's supply of Mills & Boon® books—FREE! When you're finished, simply complete the coupon overleaf and send it to us by 31st December 1998. The first five correct entries will each win a year's subscription to the Mills & Boon series of their choice. What could be easier?

Please turn over for details of how to enter

F8C

HOW TO ENTER

Simply study the two pictures overleaf. They may at first glance appear the same but look closely and you should start to see the differences. There are ten to find in total, so circle them as you go on the second picture. Finally, fill in the coupon below and pop this page into an envelope and post it today. Don't forget you could win a year's supply of Mills & Boon® books—you don't even need to pay for a stamp!

Mills & Boon Spot the Difference Competition
FREEPOST CN81, Croydon, Surrey, CR9 3WZ
EIRE readers: (please affix stamp) PO Box 4546, Dublin 24.

Please tick the series you would like to receive if you are one of the lucky winners

Presents™ ❑ Enchanted™ ❑ Medical Romance™ ❑
Historical Romance™ ❑ Temptation® ❑

Are you a Reader Service™ subscriber? Yes ❑ No ❑

Ms/Mrs/Miss/Mr ....Initials .(BLOCK CAPITALS PLEASE)

Surname...

Address ....

....

...............................Postcode...........................

(I am over 18 years of age)   F8C

Closing date for entries is 31st December 1998.
One application per household. Competition open to residents of the UK and Ireland only. You may be mailed with offers from other reputable companies as a result of this application. If you would prefer not to receive such offers, please tick this box. ❑

Mills & Boon is a registered trademark
owned by Harlequin Mills & Boon Limited.

MILLS & BOON®

Elizabeth Gage

The Collection

A compelling read of three full-length novels by
best-selling author of *A Glimpse of Stocking*

Intimate

Number One

A Stranger to Love

"...Gage is a writer of style and intelligence..."
—Chicago Tribune

On sale from 13th July 1998   Price £5.25

*Available at most branches of WH Smith, John Menzies,
Martins, Tesco, Asda, and Volume One*

Penny Jordan

COLLECTOR'S EDITION

The *Penny Jordan Collector's Edition* is
a selection of her most popular stories,
published in beautifully designed volumes
for you to collect and cherish.

*Available from Tesco, Asda, WH Smith, John Menzies,
Martins and all good paperback stockists, at £3.10 each -
or the special price of £2.80 if you use the coupon below.
On sale from 1st June 1998.*

Valid only in the UK & Eire against purchases made in retail outlets and not in
conjunction with any Reader Service or other offer.